What kind of man was he?

A normal healthy man, with all a normal healthy male's wants and needs. But Jeannie wasn't the kind of woman a man took for a night's pleasure and rode away from with a smile on his lips. She was the kind a man took home to introduce to his crazy family. She was the kind of woman a man built sun porches for, took day jobs for, settled down for.

And he wasn't that kind of a man. He was a federal marshal, a rogue, an independent rider who went his own way at the end of a job and left the pretty ranch owner in the fading sunlight.

And that was the biggest bunch of baloney he'd ever spouted to himself in his whole vagabond life.

Dear Reader,

July is a sizzling month both outside *and* in, and once again we've rounded up six exciting titles to keep your temperature rising. It all starts with the latest addition to Marilyn Pappano's HEARTBREAK CANYON miniseries, *Lawman's Redemption,* in which a brooding man needs help connecting with the lonely young girl who just might be his daughter—and he finds it in the form of a woman with similar scars in her romantic past. Don't miss this emotional, suspenseful read.

Eileen Wilks provides the next installment in our twelve-book miniseries, ROMANCING THE CROWN, with *Her Lord Protector.* Fireworks ensue when a Montebellan lord has to investigate a beautiful commoner who may be a friend—or a foe!—of the royal family. This miniseries just gets more and more intriguing. And Kathleen Creighton finishes up her latest installment of her INTO THE HEARTLAND miniseries with *The Black Sheep's Baby.* A freewheeling photojournalist who left town years ago returns— with a little pink bundle strapped to his chest, and a beautiful attorney in hot pursuit. In Marilyn Tracy's *Cowboy Under Cover,* a grief-stricken widow who has set up a haven for children in need of rescue finds herself with that same need—and her rescuer is a handsome federal marshal posing as a cowboy. Nina Bruhns is back with *Sweet Revenge,* the story of a straitlaced woman posing as her wild identical twin—and now missing—sister to learn of her fate, who in the process hooks up with the seductive detective who is also searching for her. And in *Bachelor in Blue Jeans* by Lauren Nichols, during a bachelor auction, a woman inexplicably bids on the man who once spurned her, and wins—or does she? This reunion romance will break your heart.

So get a cold drink, sit down, put your feet up and enjoy them all— and don't forget to come back next month for more of the most exciting romance reading around…only in Silhouette Intimate Moments.

Yours,

Leslie J. Wainger
Executive Senior Editor

Please address questions and book requests to:
Silhouette Reader Service
U.S.: 3010 Walden Ave., P.O. Box 1325, Buffalo, NY 14269
Canadian: P.O. Box 609, Fort Erie, Ont. L2A 5X3

Cowboy Under Cover
MARILYN TRACY

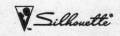

INTIMATE MOMENTS™

Published by Silhouette Books

America's Publisher of Contemporary Romance

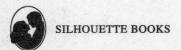

SILHOUETTE BOOKS

ISBN 0-373-27232-4

COWBOY UNDER COVER

Copyright © 2002 by Tracy LeCocq

This edition published by arrangement with Harlequin Books S.A.

® and TM are trademarks of Harlequin Books S.A., used under license.
Trademarks indicated with ® are registered in the United States Patent
and Trademark Office, the Canadian Trade Marks Office and in other
countries.

Visit Silhouette at www.eHarlequin.com

Printed in U.S.A.

MARILYN TRACY

lives in Portales, New Mexico, in a ramshackle turn-of-the-century house with her son, two dogs, three cats and a poltergeist. Between remodeling the house to its original Victorian-cum-Deco state, writing full-time and finishing a forty-foot cement dragon in the backyard, Marilyn composes full soundtracks to go with each of her novels.

After having lived in both Tel Aviv and Moscow in conjunction with the U.S. State Department, Marilyn enjoys writing about the cultures she's explored and the people she's grown to love. She likes to hear from people who enjoy her books and always has a pot of coffee on or a glass of wine ready for anyone dropping by, especially if they don't mind chaos and know how to wield a paintbrush.

For my loving family, by birth and by choice, who sticks with me through experimental food nights, emotional upheavals and my addiction to happy endings.

Chapter 1

Chance Salazar was chewing the fat with Doreen Gallegos across the scarred wooden countertop of the Carlsbad post office when a stranger walked in.

Doreen flicked a glance at the newcomer and leaned close enough to Chance that he could have drowned in her musky perfume, but she didn't lower her voice. "Mama will be at church bingo tonight, and you could come over. The kids'll be with Geo. We can talk."

Chance muttered something noncommittal, his eyes on the woman standing at the Wait Here sign. She was taller than most women, almost six feet, and her lush curves were only partially concealed by her obviously new blue jeans and chambray shirt. She'd pulled her curly, longish auburn hair into a rough ponytail, revealing her elegant neck and a host of Irish freckles. She reminded him of a roan Appaloosa filly he'd once coveted. And everything about her—from her new duds to her designer sunglasses—let him know she wasn't from anywhere near Carlsbad, New Mexico. Was she a tourist to see the caverns?

She held a manila envelope in one hand and a slender notepad in the other. She flipped the notebook open.

"What about it, Chance?" Doreen asked. "I made some sangria yesterday. Good burgundy, four lemons, two oranges, three limes and plenty of time to steep. And I want to talk to you about…you know."

The woman tucked the envelope beneath her arm and wrote something in the notepad. A small smile played around her full lips.

"I made a whole gallon. And I got ice this morning. And Mama made tamales last night, so you wouldn't have to worry about finding something for dinner."

"Customer, Doreen," Chance said, stepping back from the counter and smiling at the woman. She didn't smile back. Unfriendly? Or was she not looking at him? Impossible to tell with her eyes covered.

"You wait right there, Chance," Doreen commanded, pointing at the wall. She didn't take her eyes off him until he leaned back and crossed his arms. Only then did she look at the woman and add with a note of impatience, "Can I help you?"

The woman started, as if surprised awake, then moved to the counter. She set the notebook to the side. "I need some information," she said. Her voice held no trace of a southwest twang. When Doreen didn't say anything, the woman smiled and handed across the thick envelope, "And stamps for this, please."

Doreen held up the envelope. "How you want it?"

"I beg your pardon?"

"How do you want it to go?" Doreen asked, filling in the words as if speaking to a second grader. "First class? Express? Overnight?'' Doreen looked at the address. "Washington, D.C., that'd be twelve dollars for an overnight express, but no guarantees because it's already past ten. Overnights have to be in by nine if you want to be sure it gets there the next day, and even then, I can't make you no promises, because who knows what some idiot is going to do down the line somewhere, right? Two-day air is the safest bet and not so expensive. Still, if you want to go on the cheap, you can send it bulk. So, how you want it?''

"Two-day air will be fine,'' the woman said. In contrast to Doreen's staccato soprano, the newcomer sounded as if she were speaking in contralto slow motion. "And thanks.''

"No problemo. What else?''

Chance leaned forward and tilted his head a little to read what the stranger had been writing in her notepad. *Fires. Spontaneous combustion? Lightning? What kind of animal destroys fences? Find out difference between ranch hand and cowboy? Where are the cattle? Chance—cowboy name? Hispanic name? Pass, Carlsbad style—Mama's playing church bingo. Recipe for sangria—four lemons, two oranges, three limes to one gallon burgundy. Let steep.*

As if aware he was reading her notes, or perhaps simply preparing to leave, the woman pulled the notepad to her chest. "And, I need to know where to find a police station.''

"Something wrong?'' Doreen asked.

The woman's shoulders stiffened slightly. Chance suspected she was unused to being questioned by strangers. If she planned on staying in New Mexico long, she'd have to get over that. People in these parts discussed others' business more often than they did their own. She pulled her sunglasses from her eyes. Even from his spot against the wall, viewing her profile only, Chance could see how blue her eyes were. Summer-sky blue. And wary.

Contrary to her generally hard facade, Doreen was, as Chance knew, a sensitive woman, and he wasn't surprised when she stepped back a pace, as if trouble were contagious. "The police station's across the street about three blocks up." She pointed west. The woman followed her finger and narrowed her eyes against the bright, if dusty, window. "And then, for big stuff, like drug runners and such, you want the federal marshal's office, and that's around the corner and east about three blocks and upstairs and you can tell Ted Peters that Doreen sent you. But, if you're having a problem out at Milagro, you're gonna want the sheriff."

When the woman didn't explain why she needed a peace officer, Doreen continued, "Police for city, sheriff for county, same as most everywhere, I guess. 'Cept the sheriff's elected. And he's across the plaza at the courthouse. Nando Gallegos. He's a cousin."

"How did you know—"

"That you're from Rancho Milagro?" Doreen grinned with the old gamine mischief that had gotten her in trouble so many times when Chance knew her in high school—and maybe a version of the same smile that landed her with three kids and two divorces before she was twenty-two, and a host of debts, worries and at least a handful of bad relationships since. She held up the woman's envelope and waggled it. "It's on the return."

The tension in the woman's shoulder's eased. "Of course," she said, and with her lack of west Texas drawl and her clear consonants, she sounded as if she'd stepped straight from a presidential tea. "Thank you for your help. And the sheriff's your cousin, you say?"

"Fernando. But everybody calls him Nando. Tell him I sent you over there. Doreen Gallegos. He'll help you out with whatever your problem is, okay?"

Chance withheld a derisive snort. Nando Gallegos was the biggest jerk this side of the Mississippi River.

The woman smiled, murmured a thank-you for the third time since she'd entered the post office, paid for her two-day overnight mail and left the small lobby, all without looking at the wall where Chance rested his shoulder. All without looking at him, in other words, he thought wryly. Chance saw her stop outside the threshold, slip her sunglasses on and jot something down. He smiled. It was oddly pleasant to think his name was already in her little notepad.

"So?" Doreen asked. "What do *you* want, Chance?"

"Did she seem like she's in trouble, Doreen?" he asked, pushing off the wall and joining her at the counter.

Doreen sighed. "Men. They're all alike. A pretty new face, and the old one's forgotten just like that." She snapped her fingers.

Chance smiled at her. "Really, Doreen?"

She tried maintaining the miffed look, but giggled instead and slapped at his arm. "You're the worst of them all, Chance Salazar. You only think of two things—fast horses and faster women."

"But not necessarily in that order," he said, flicking her cheek with a finger. He grinned at her easily, knowing she wasn't at all vulnerable to his flirting, but recognizing that their long-past history and Doreen's many heartaches, and knowing that dalliance kept her fear of loneliness at bay, Chance played the game with her.

They had been friends for far too long not to be totally honest with one another—at least about relationships. Besides, Doreen was desperately, almost painfully in love with one of the boys at the federal marshal's office and had confided this to Chance when he'd come back to Carlsbad a few months earlier.

Her hard little features softened into a genuine look of affection, one Chance suspected she reserved only for her family and him. "What you need, Chance, is to fall in love." She held up her hand to forestall his wisecrack. "I mean really in love. Maybe then you'd know what the rest of us feel like every day."

"Miserable and full of self-doubt?" he quipped.

She gave him a long look and nodded. "Maybe. Or maybe happy. You know a whole bunch about laughing, but I don't think you know so much about feeling happy inside."

"Doreen, I'm going to start having to pay you for the couch advice."

She sniffed. "You could do worse. I'm not the one who rides bucking horses for a living and then goes and breaks my collarbone. Now get out of here and let me go to work. And if you happen to stop by the marshal's office…"

"And just happen to run into Ted Peters…"

"You can tell any one of them that their box rent is due," she said primly.

"I'll do that, Doreen," he said. "And thanks for the invite for sangria and tamales."

"Don't tell me, I know. You've got another bone to break."

He grinned at her and tipped his hat. He was reaching for the door handle when she called after him, "Her name is Jeannie McMunn. She's one of the new owners at Rancho Milagro."

"Get all that from the return address?" he asked.

"Give me some credit, Chance Salazar. I knew who she was a month ago. She's got two other partners who are still back east, she's done a lot of repairs out at Milagro—she's spent a fortune, which nobody knows where it came from—and she's turning the place into some kind of orphan's ranch. She hired a couple to be her house- and groundskeepers, Juanita and Tomás Montoya, you know them?"

Chance shook his head.

Doreen shrugged. "They came up from Mexico after you left, I guess. Somebody told me they used to work up in Roswell at Job Corps."

Chance gave a low whistle. "Ted Peters better watch out. You know as much as the Feds do."

"That's not all I know," Doreen said, leaning across the counter. This time she did lower her voice. "I know what her trouble is."

Chance stepped into the cool post office lobby. "What is it?"

"Nobody told her Rancho Milagro is haunted. Really, Chance. Nando was telling me about it the other night at Juana's first communion party. The party where you were so busy making up to my cousin Lucinda."

"I guess we're pretty lucky to have a sheriff who believes in ghosts. Maybe that'll help him find Lucinda's husband. He can hold a séance and some voice will tell him where Jorge disappeared to."

"Scoff all you want, Chance, but I'm telling you that's what's troubling this Jeannie McMunn. Nando told me all about it. Strange lights in the sky, spooky sounds. Maybe that's why they call the place Rancho Milagro.''

"*Milagro* means miracle, not ghost, remember? Ghost Ranch is up north, Georgia O'Keeffe's ranch.''

"Spirits, miracles…whatever. I can tell you this, I don't want to see either one, God forgive me,'' she said, swiftly making the sign of the cross. "Me? I believe the old stories.'' She sighed. "*Pobrecita.* Out there all alone. No husband. No friends.''

"Give her some time, Doreen. She's only been here a little while.''

"What do you suppose she meant by writing that business about spontaneous combustion in her notebook?''

Chance pushed his hat back and raised his eyebrows at her. "You read upside down in addition to your other talents, Doreen?'' he asked.

"Anyone who works at the post office does. It's part of our job. Besides, I saw you reading it, too, and I never heard tell of any bronc rider who needed to read other people's stuff.''

Jeannie McMunn turned the air-conditioning in the new Jeep Cherokee to maximum and leaned forward to draw in the blast of cold air. She felt wilted by the heat—''a hundred and five hot degrees in the shade of Grandma's apple tree,'' the radio weatherman had called it. She didn't doubt it whatsoever. She'd sit here and absorb all the cold she could before driving the few short blocks to the courthouse to talk with the sheriff—Nando Gallegos, cousin of Doreen, the postal clerk.

She thought about the letter she'd mailed, on a two-day overnight status, no less. In just two days, Leeza and Corrie, her best friends in the world, her family of choice and her mainstays in a life gone crazy, would be opening the biggest pack of lies she'd ever told—except for the lies she'd told the day her husband, David, and baby Angela were killed. She'd told them everything was fine that day, too, that she would survive. That she'd be okay in time.

In the letter she'd given Doreen to mail for her, she'd once again said all was well. She'd told them the ranch renovations were completed—and hadn't mentioned she'd run afoul of inspectors who had blood vendettas with contractors and who wouldn't sign off on that contractor's work and that only a few judicious bribes, much pleading and in two instances hiring of other contractors had resulted in Rancho Milagro's okay for final inspection.

She'd told them it finally rained, but didn't add that when the downpour came, lightning struck the prairie and started grass fires and that a wall of muddy water flash flooded the new dirt road that cost a fortune to grade in the first place.

And she'd written that the state had finally approved their status as a foster-care ranch, not bothering to mention that their plan of becoming a full-care facility for orphans wouldn't become a reality until such time as hell apparently froze over or another inspector's feud with some other warring family might end, whichever came first.

And she'd said their first two foster children were charming. This was perhaps the biggest lie of all. One had arrived at the ranch some thirty miles north of Carlsbad all alone and without a scrap of paperwork and refused to—or couldn't—speak. A host of doctors, speaking both English and Spanish, had examined the boy and found no physical reason for the silence, and no governmental agency could lay claim to him. He was a mystery in every sense of the word.

And the other child, a girl of fifteen going on forty, with an attitude bigger than the Washington Monument, had been passed from one foster-care situation to another and, as far as Jeannie could see, hated the entire world and every single member of its population, with her newest guardian, Jeannie McMunn, heading the long list.

Leeza and Corrie would see right through her cheery web of lies. They always did. She moaned, leaning her head against the steering wheel. They knew her too well. They would read between every line, see every falsehood and then would call her on the cell phone and send endless amounts of e-mail—which she didn't have to worry about, as the phones at the ranch weren't connected yet. At least she didn't have to explain away the lack of telephone lines. This lack was logical. No wires had been attached to the canted telephone poles running beside the road leading to the ranch.

But within two days of receiving the letter, one of them would hop on a plane and come see what had happened to her dear, demented friend.

She'd turned the letter over to Doreen only moments ago. She could get it back. She could stop the lies, stop the questions and most of all stop her friends from coming to check on her. Jeannie drew in a final deep breath of cold air, turned off the Jeep and leaped from the vehicle onto the heat-slammed Carlsbad street. Whatever temperature it might be in the weatherman's grandmother's apple-tree shade, the asphalt in downtown Carlsbad added at least another five degrees to the August heat. It was hot enough to kill.

She broke into a run, ducking the sun, fumbling with her sunglasses, muttering imprecations about her evil, lying ways, and ran into a wall.

"Steady there," a drawling baritone voice said as strong hands grasped her shoulders and held her before she could reel backward. She told herself it was too little sleep and too many concerns that made her slow to react. She had oddest urge to close her eyes and pretend the sensation of this man's protection was real. Her eyelids fluttered shut, seemingly of their own volition.

"Are you okay, ma'am?" He had a voice like corduroy, soft and rough at the same time.

She opened her eyes and stared at the man-wall she'd run into, the one still holding her upper arms in his firm grasp. Chance. The cowboy in the post office. The man Doreen had invited over to talk with because her mama was going to be at bingo that night.

He was taller than her by several inches, which put him at something over six feet four inches, and built upon strong, lean lines. A man of about forty years of age, he seemed a mix of heritage and cultures—Anglo mixed with Hispanic background, perhaps, or Native American. He was dressed Western style and his eyes were a strange green-hazel flecked with brown and made all the more striking by long, black eyelashes, and jet-black eyebrows set in a deeply tanned, chiseled face with laugh lines radiating from the creases of his eyes.

"Ma'am?" he asked.

"Oh, yes," she said, finally. "I'm fine, yes."

His eyes roved her face, almost as if he was mem-

orizing her features, but she could read nothing more
than a polite concern. She nodded, and he released her,
though he kept his hands near her shoulders for another
second or two before he slowly lowered them to his
sides.

Jeannie knew a momentary pang of regret. No matter
how foolish it might have seemed, for the first time in
the two long years without David in the world, she'd
felt a flicker of safety, as if she were being cared for.
It didn't matter how fleetingly. But, startling her, she'd
also felt something else, a stirring of a different kind,
that inexplicable tingle of chemistry between a man
and a woman.

The man with the tanned face and green eyes smiled
and held out one of the large hands that had held her
moments before, callused palm upward, long fingers
outstretched. "Chance Salazar," he said.

She almost said, "I know," as she placed her hand
in his. The shock of the contact rippled throughout her
body. She had no idea what the expression on her face
must have read, but was afraid he knew she was struggling for any words that might diffuse the impact of
his touch.

Don't forget Mama's at bingo tonight, she thought.

He hitched a shoulder, and his smile edged upward.
"Chance is a family name. It was my granddaddy's
rodeo name, now it's mine."

Had he read her notebook when it was sitting on the
counter in the post office? She flushed, trying to remember what else she'd jotted down. Leeza and Corrie
had often kidded her about the notebooks, and she'd
always replied that old habits died hard. This old habit
might have just met its maker.

But he wasn't looking at her as if amused at having read her thoughts. "And you are?"

In trouble, she thought, but said, "Jeannie Mc-Munn." With a Ph.D. in cultural anthropology, twelve years of teaching at George Washington University and a host of publications under her belt, she was generally comfortable under any circumstances. Yet she'd never felt more socially inept in her life as she did at this moment.

She briefly returned the pressure of his hand before retrieving her own. "I'm sorry about slamming into you. I wasn't paying attention to where I was going."

"Looked like you were running from a polecat," he said and, if anything, his smile increased.

"I just dropped off a letter and wanted it back. I...I forgot to add something." She couldn't have said why she felt the need to explain herself. She seldom felt the need. She generally took a logical path, and those didn't need explaining.

"That's easy enough. Doreen'll take care of it for you."

"Doreen. Yes. Weren't you in the post office a minute ago?" she asked.

"I was. I saw you in there. And since Doreen's already said something about your return address being Rancho Milagro, I won't ask where you're staying hereabouts."

She nodded and smiled. "Just as well. You're both right. I'm one of the owners of it now."

"And turning it into a children's home, I hear."

"I'm trying, anyway."

"You're braver than I am, but it's a good thing you're trying to do."

"I hope so," she said and wished her voice hadn't

sounded so wistful, as if asking him to reassure her. She'd spent the last two years being weak and hating every minute of it. She wasn't about to slip into that zone again.

"After you fetch your letter, where are you heading? There's a good little café over there. Annie's. They make a great cup of coffee." He gestured across the street, his meaning clear.

She couldn't help but smile at him, at his friendly invitation and even more engaging grin. Charm, she thought. The man oozed charm and self-confidence. But all the charm in the world wouldn't make her ready to spend time with a man again. She shook her head. "I'm afraid not," she said. "I've some errands."

"Right," he said, accepting the tacit rejection with grace. "When I was a kid and we lived out on the ranch, we'd make weekly runs to town and spend most of the day just trying to catch up with ourselves." He looked as if he might say more, then lifted a finger to the brim of his straw cowboy hat and grinned at her. "It was a pleasure meeting you, Jeannie McMunn, and I hope to see you around again soon."

"Thank you, Mr. Salazar."

"Chance."

"Chance. And I'm sorry again for running into you."

"I'm not," he said, and the look in his eyes made her heart give a little jolt. "But you better get in out of this sun before you drop dead from heatstroke." He reached around her and opened the door of the post office. Ice-cold air billowed into the street, creating a mirage effect that rippled in the air between them.

"Thank you," she said weakly.

"You're most welcome. And listen, if you need anything, you just holler, okay? Anyone knows where to find me around here.''

''I will,'' she said, stepping beneath his upraised arm, wondering how he could wear a starched cotton long sleeve shirt in this kind of heat, and worse, wondering how he could smell so good when all he smelled like was sunshine and fresh soap.

He let the door swing shut behind her, and she stood for several seconds just inside the post office, gulping in refrigerated air and wishing Doreen the postal clerk wasn't watching her with such a knowing smile on her pretty little face.

Chapter 2

Chance watched the door of the post office from his table at Annie's café. Doreen must have been probing for information, for it took more than fifteen minutes for Jeannie McMunn to reappear in the hot sunlight. She looked bemused, he thought, as well she should after spending time with Doreen, but she also wore a faint smile on her lips.

Chance hoped the smile might mean the start of a friendship between the newcomer and Doreen. He knew for a fact that Doreen needed a girlfriend, a person she could be as comfortable with as she was with him. And he suspected Jeannie McMunn needed someone, too. The clues lay in the shadows in her blue eyes, the darker circles beneath them that told of sleepless nights.

The café's phone rang, and the owner, Annie Davis, called that it was for Chance. "It's Doreen," she said, handing the receiver across the crowded countertop.

Resting his elbow between the pies and the fresh rolls, he watched as Jeannie McMunn stepped up into her Jeep and smiled when she leaned into the air-conditioning vents. "What do you need, kiddo?" he asked Doreen.

She gave a swift account of her conversation with Jeannie, ending it with Jeannie's itinerary for the remainder of the morning.

"And I'm supposed to waylay her on these rounds?" he asked and chuckled aloud at Doreen's resounding affirmative.

"She tell you what the trouble was at the ranch?"

Doreen said no as Chance watched Jeannie put the Jeep into reverse and slowly back out into the street.

"You told her the newspaper office was where?" Chance asked, then laughed aloud when Doreen explained her less than understandable directions. "And I'm supposed to rescue her and steer her in the right direction? Is that your plot?"

He no sooner rang off than he tossed a couple of dollar bills onto the counter, called a goodbye to Annie and was out the door. By cutting down an alley and across an empty lot on the south side of the River Walk, he was standing in front of the old theater before Jeannie McMunn pulled into a spot directly in front of him.

"Now this must be my lucky day," he drawled as she jumped from the Jeep.

She stopped and eyed him warily. She looked from him to the obviously empty building behind him. "And this, I take it, is not the newspaper office."

He looked around as if surprised at her question. "Why, no, ma'am. It's the theater. Not that it's open anymore. They have one of those multiplex jobs out at the mall. And no one seemed to want to watch the B-string movies small-town theaters are only allowed nowadays.''

She reached for the car door.

"How about something cold to drink?" he asked. When she turned to face him, her mouth ready for a denial, he continued swiftly, "No coffee, but summer errands always run smoother on something cold."

"You're fairly persistent, aren't you, Mr. Salazar?"

"You've no idea, Ms. McMunn."

"I'm sure you have better things to do with your time," she said.

"No, ma'am, that I don't."

She cocked her head at him as if trying to guess his measure. He smiled at her. She shook her head. "What do you do, Mr. Salazar?"

"Chance."

"What do you do, Chance?"

For half a second, he almost told her the truth. He found he inexplicably wanted to, but the lie was both protection and second nature to him. "Ride the rodeo," he said. "Broncs mostly."

"You ride in rodeos?"

He smiled at her phrasing. "Yes, ma'am, I do. But since there doesn't seem to be a rodeo on at the moment, I'd just as soon buy a pretty lady an iced tea over at Annie's café."

She gave him a long, cool look of appraisal then seemed to reach a decision. "All right. On one condition."

"Fair enough," he said. "I have to hear it before I agree to it."

She chuckled, and he felt a twinge inside. "My condition is that you'll play guide to my errands. I tried following Doreen's instructions and wound up here, as you can see.''

''You were heading for the newspaper office, I take it?''

She smiled. ''That's right.''

''And then the sheriff's?''

''The sheriff's?''

''You asked about it in the post office.''

''Right. The sheriff's. Yes. Actually, maybe I should go there first and then the newspaper. One might preclude the other.''

''Because the sheriff might be able to solve a problem for you.''

She stiffened. ''I—yes. Maybe.''

''Nobody's been bothering you, have they?'' he asked.

She hesitated, clearly torn.

''They have,'' he said. ''And that's why you need to talk with Nando.'' Instead of questioning her further, which obviously made her uncomfortable, he lifted a hand to her shoulder and gently propelled her so she stood in the opening of her car door. ''Hop in, and we'll head out. It's only a block or so from here, but at this time of day, in this heat, it's not a good idea to walk very far.''

She smiled at him. ''Especially if you're not used to it.''

''Especially then,'' he agreed. He waited until she'd fastened her seat belt and started her Jeep before shutting her door and walking around to the passenger side. The simple action felt oddly intimate, as if he were protecting her. As he adjusted his seat belt, he couldn't help noticing Annie and Doreen standing at the end of the alley a block over, watching them and talking animatedly.

And looking to his left and up, he saw Ted Peters standing in the window of the federal marshal's office watching Doreen and Annie. He shook his head.

"Which way?" Jeannie asked.

"Pull out and go left about a block, to the plaza. The sheriff's office is in the courthouse."

"Do you know him well?"

"Nando? Sure. I grew up around here, and it's a pretty small place. Turn right here and park in the shade of that tree."

She did as he instructed then hesitated over the key. She wanted to see the sheriff alone, he thought, and didn't know quite how to tell him. "Better go ahead and turn it off," he said. "Even though I'll be right here, cars can overheat in a big hurry in these parts."

She flashed him a smile filled with such relief, he realized he'd misunderstood her hesitation. She didn't know him from Adam, and though she'd agreed to let him guide her around Carlsbad that afternoon, she wasn't ready to leave her new Jeep in a stranger's possession. Good for her, he thought. A little distrust was a healthy thing.

She lowered the windows before cutting the engine, smiled at him again, took her handbag and soon disappeared into the pueblo-style courthouse.

A little distrust or no, he wished she'd told him what her trouble was. After several glances at the slim notebook lying on the seat, he sighed and picked it up. He flipped the cover over and began reading her notes. By the time he reached his name, he knew a healthy bit about her woes at Rancho Milagro. And cursed himself for not warning her that Nando Gallegos would be about as much help as inviting a fox over for dinner in the henhouse.

Sheriff Fernando Gallegos lay back in his chair like Jabba the Hut sprawled on his mound of cushions in one of the *Star Wars* movies. The sheriff's large belly rose above the surface of his desk as an independent land mass, and his fleshy hands played with his ornate belt buckle. He was the antithesis of the man waiting for her in her Jeep and looked nothing like his petite cousin Doreen.

It took Jeannie less than three minutes to seriously question the minds of the voters in Eddy County. In those short minutes, Sheriff Fernando Gallegos dismissed the fence cutting as the work of pranksters and the fires on her prairie as unfortunate results of recent lightning storms. He managed to look a little more concerned about her missing herd of cattle, but told her with thickly accented patronage that they probably just wandered off in search of greener grass.

"We've had a drought, you know. What's that nursery rhyme? 'Leave 'em alone, and they'll come home?' Something like that. You catching my meaning, missy?"

He did make one thing very clear, however. He was not going to launch anything resembling an investigation.

"Sounds to me like you need to hire some ranch hands, missy," he suggested. He looked at her with sudden speculation that nonetheless seemed coldly calculating. "Tell you what. I know some boys who would be just perfect for you. One of them's even a cousin. No relation to Doreen. I'll have them drive on out there and take care of your little problems for you. How's that sound?''

Jeannie smiled though her heart sank. She couldn't imagine appreciating anyone this man would recommend. She thought of the cowboy sitting in her car. Could he help? She had the irrational feeling he would know exactly what to do about broken fences, prairie fires and missing cattle.

"It'll take me a couple of days to round my boys up, but I'll send them along your way then. How's that sound?''

She wanted to tell him that, like his other suggestions, it sounded dreadfully lacking in official support. He was the sheriff and the law. The way he called them "my boys" sounded too paternal to her Eastern ears. This wasn't the Wild West anymore, was it?

"'Course, you could put an ad in the local paper and see what kind of riffraff you get." He laughed at the notion.

She stifled the jolt his words gave her. There was no way on earth he could know she had already drafted just such an ad. She thought of the notebook resting on the seat of her Jeep and thought of the cowboy in the same car. Chance.

He continued, "Do you speak Spanish? Most likely all you'd get would be wetbacks who won't speak a word of English and rob you blind in the process."

Her dislike of Sheriff Nando Gallegos escalated more than several notches. His prejudice made her stiffen her spine and lift her chin.

"Or you might get a couple of boys who just want to get in good with you, marry-the-boss types. A pretty lady can get kinda itchy way out there by herself. I can think of a couple of lowlifes hereabouts who wouldn't mind putting in a little time for some big rewards. You get my meaning?''

Jeannie held back a shudder, not so much at his crass suggestion, but at the notion that he would make it at all.

''You'd be much better off taking the boys I send you. You'd have to pay them, of course, but they'd answer to me. Better that way. Besides, you'd be doing me a big favor. My cousin's living at my sister's place now, driving her plumb crazy, and she's ready for him to move out.'' He fidgeted with his silver belt buckle, lightly polishing it with his forefinger. ''Anything else now?''

Since he wasn't willing to drive the thirty miles to check out her report, there was little else she could imagine needing from the sheriff, especially the cousin the sheriff's sister didn't want around the house. She shook her head and waited as he pushed himself from his sprung chair to walk her to the door.

He held her hand two seconds too long, his beady gaze unsettling. ''You'll be hearing from my boys real soon.''

The heat of the burning street seemed a welcome relief from the damp cool of the sheriff's office. And seeing Chance Salazar patiently waiting in her Jeep made the last few minutes seem surreal. He pushed her door open and smiled at her as she climbed into the driver's seat.

''All fixed?'' he asked.

She shook her head and found, to her disgust, her hand was shaking as she tried inserting the key into the ignition. The nervous reaction was as much about her disgust with the sheriff as it was proximity to one good-looking cowboy taking up far too much room in the front of her Jeep.

"Newspaper office next?" he asked.

"Yes," she said. "Definitely."

"It's a good paper, but I've never heard anyone want to get hold of it with quite that passion."

She chuckled. "I need to place an ad."

"In that case, go left, left again at the next corner, and it'll be on your right about three blocks from there."

"We'll end up at the theater again."

"Trust me," he said.

She looked at him and found him gazing directly at her. He wasn't smiling.

"Trust me," he said again. His voice was a caress, and his eyes held a fathomless depth.

Her heart fumbled a beat. How could she trust him? Even on such a small thing as directions? She couldn't trust anything anymore. Her days of trust were buried in a cemetery in Virginia.

"Please?" he asked.

"Okay," she said, "On directions, I think I will." He'd never know what an admission even that small concession was, nor how frightening.

Chapter 3

"Get a load of this, man," Pablo Garcia said, rattling the newspaper as he folded it to the classified section. "It's here, just like Annie over at the café said. 'Cowboys needed.' I'll bet it's that Rancho Milagro."

Chance grunted and slapped at a fly made slow by the coolness of the early August morning. He didn't look up from his mountain of paperwork. The hours between five and eight in the morning were the only time he could tackle the onerous job. The rest of the time he was busy playacting the rodeo king.

He grinned when one of his men asked Pablo, "You have a hankering to work all of a sudden?"

Two of the other men in the federal marshal's office chuckled, but Pablo ignored the gibe. A valuable informant, quasi-private investigator and sometime chauffeur, Pablo was the general man Friday at the marshal's outpost in Carlsbad. The fact that he was related to a good half of the Carlsbad district's population—including Chance Salazar—made him near priceless.

"No, guys, listen," Pablo said, his Hispanic accent thickening in his interest. "Says here, 'cowboys needed. Room, board—what's that, food?—salary and a horse provided. Experience with all facets of ranching required. Background with children a plus. Position to begin immediately.' And there's a phone number and a box number at the paper."

One of the other men, Dell Johnson, a tall drink of water with a blond moustache, chuckled. "Translated that means sleeping on the floor, eating a bowl of beans and some dried-out tortillas and riding the worst old range horse this side of the Pecos."

"Probably has mange," Ted Peters, another deputy, agreed. He was as dark as Dell Johnson was fair and was built like a football player. At least, that was what Doreen claimed.

Chance continued his paperwork, not joining in the other men's chiding of Pablo for believing the advertisement. He believed it, too. He'd been with Jeannie McMunn when she placed the ridiculous thing. He'd seen the rough draft of the ad in her notebook, the receipt for the ad when she paid for it and a printout of what was, in his opinion, an invitation for certain disaster.

He'd spent that night with a bottle of eighty-proof guilt for not telling the truth and for having let her spill her troubles to Nando Gallegos. Chance was dead certain the duly elected sheriff wouldn't have done a thing to help the pretty woman with the long red hair and the bluest eyes he'd ever seen.

The things he'd read in Jeannie McMunn's notebook, the hints Doreen had offered, the few tidbits

Jeannie had let drop that day he'd squired her around town and several days of gossiping since let him know the new rancher had several serious problems worrying her. She had a herd of missing cattle, cut fences—which might or might not explain the lost cows—and someone was setting grass fires. Lightning might often strike twice, but it seldom created systematic fires.

And Chance would lay good money on the odds that *El Patron* was behind her woes. A self-made emperor, the man answered to no one, least of all the law. In fact, it was widely known that at least part of the law in Carlsbad, one Sheriff Fernando Gallegos, worked for *El Patron*.

Unlike the other men in the marshal's office, Chance had spent the Friday evening before at a barbecue celebrating his rodeo and contractor buddy's successful completion of the renovations at Rancho Milagro. After a few Tecates, his friend had waxed ecstatic about the amount of money the rich women from back East had shelled out trying to turn the ranch headquarters into a working children's home.

Chance was fairly certain his friend, Charlie Budacher, hadn't abused the women's trust, but at the same time, Chance would have to have been blindly loyal not to see that his friend had offered no discounts whatsoever. Still, according to Charlie, renovation of the old historic if broken down ranch headquarters hadn't been any picnic. A couple more beers, and his friend had revealed that he suspected somebody of nasty shenanigans at Rancho Milagro.

"You ask me, it's no miracle ranch, but a cursed one. Poor thing, out there all by her lonesome. She's a real looker, too—don't tell Annie I said that, she'd close up the café and move to Florida or somewhere and then where would I get breakfast and a date on Saturday nights? Something sad about her, though. That Jeannie McMunn, I mean. Anyway, I'd sure hate to see *El Patron* and his lowlifes drive that redhead out of there."

Chance would hate to see that, too, though he suspected it might be better if the woman packed up and moved home. The trouble was, he didn't want to see her leave. He liked the way she smiled, as if not real sure the expression belonged on her face. He liked the way she jotted stuff down in that silly little notebook then left it lying around for anyone to read. And he admired what she was trying to do out there. If more people took an interest in the lost kids of the world, maybe the world would be a better place.

Or maybe he was just attracted to her.

"Hell, I'm outta here pretty soon," said Jack Dawson, the oldest of the marshal's crew, who was slated for retirement in a matter of weeks and current acting marshal in the office. "Gimme that ad, maybe I'll apply. Supplement the dinky bit the government calls a pension."

"You on a horse? This I gotta see," Ted quipped before grabbing a pen to simulate a microphone and lowering his voice to mimic a golf announcer's near murmur. "We see Jack Dawson stepping up to the saddle now, folks. He's never touched a creature this big before and he pauses for a moment to take in the sheer awesome size of the horse. Ah, he knows what he needs now and is bringing out the airplane ramp. Yes, ladies and gentlemen, we have a pro here today."

Chance grinned over his papers as the entire crew, including Jack, laughed at the jab on Jack's passion for golf.

But Pablo wasn't finished. The only one of the federal marshal's crew without a master's degree in criminal justice, he never lost sight of the fact that the growth potential for a general man Friday wasn't great. "I could be a cowboy. I can *vaquero* with the best of them. Hell, I was practically weaned on a horse. You tell them, Chance," he said, then chuckled. "Besides, you all have to admit, I'm pretty good with a mustang."

"As long as it has four on the floor and six little ponies under the hood," Dell quipped.

"You think this is for real, boss?" Pablo asked.

Chance mumbled an assent and signed the last of his papers. "Quit calling me boss. And yeah, it's for real. It's nuts, but it's for real."

Ted said, "They'll have every damned macho outlaw for seventeen counties showing up at their door. What the heck were they thinking, placing such an ad?"

Chance put the papers into his out box for Jack's secretary to deal with when she came in later that morning. She thought the rodeo rider, Chance Salazar, only came around for coffee, doughnuts and some lighthearted flirting with her. By the time she came to work, he'd be lounging against the wall, looking for all the world as if he'd just arrived. "It's a ranch, they need hands," he said.

"Phones must be ringing off the hook."

Chance smiled. "After she placed the ad the other day, I dropped in on Pete Griego over at the phone company. He said his boys had the poles ready, but after we chatted, I don't think they're in any big rush to get them strung. The ranch won't be getting very many calls."

Dell gave a low whistle. "I'd hate to have you on my bad side, buddy. You know half the damned county. You gotta tell me, what made Pete think an itinerant rodeo cowboy should be telling him what to do?"

Chance grinned. "He volunteered."

"And why would he do that?"

"Because we go way back."

"I swear, Chance, you and everybody else in this whole blamed state go way back," Dell said.

"If he's not related to them," Ted interjected. "Or Pablo here."

"I happened to meet the new owner of Rancho Milagro the other day. Showed her around town a little bit," Chance said.

Dell whistled again, "Pretty?"

Chance felt the back of his neck grow hot despite the air-conditioned office. "I'd say she is definitely that, yes."

"And of course, you needed her phone number."

The crew exchanged knowing grins, and Jack groaned. "And just like that, Pete blurted out all the information the phone company has on her."

"Something along those lines."

"You know, you're wasted as a federal marshal, Chance. The CIA could use you," Dell said in awed tones.

"What beats me is how every woman in town still loves you even when you move on to someone else," Ted said.

Chance looked at Ted to see what ailed the young man. Surely he didn't believe the rumors they had spread about Chance Salazar. His supposed success with women was a part of his cover and fit with his reputation way back in high school. He suspected the man's note of rancor stemmed from desire for—and jealousy over—a certain little lady at the post office.

Dell answered, "Women love him because of his cover. They all know a rodeo cowboy won't amount to a hill of beans, but they think he's wild and dangerous. Women crave the adventure he represents."

"You been reading those self-help books again, Dell?" Jack queried.

Chance grinned, standing and finishing the last of his nearly cold coffee. "According to Charlie Budacher, they've been having a little trouble out at the ranch."

"Hell, that ranch is what, fourteen thousand acres, give or take, not to mention all the state land flanking it? They're bound to have some kind of trouble."

"Fence cutting, prairie fires, that sort of nonsense."

"And you're thinking it's *El Patron*'s work," Ted said astutely.

"I am," Chance affirmed.

Ted said reflectively, "Even without the phones up, with this ad, she'll be getting lots of applications through the newspaper box number, if they don't just drive out there. Everybody around here knows the remodel job is finished at Milagro, and the ad gives it away by saying they'll give preference to anyone with knowledge of kids."

"Most of the folks who would want that job wouldn't be able to write. Besides, most folks around here all know that *El Patron* considers that his personal playground," Jack said.

Ted asked, "Why is that, anyway? The rangeland's not that hot, it's a fair distance from the border, with sinkholes that probably hook up with the caverns. He could have bought it when it was up for sale, anyhow. So why does he want to mess with it now?"

Pablo offered an answer. "He's real superstitious, *El Patron* is. My grandfather used to tell a story about some kind of magic spring on Rancho Milagro."

"I suppose it makes people live forever," Jack murmured.

"No, it makes wishes come true."

"So why didn't *El Patron* buy the place? The creep is loaded."

"That man don't pay money for nothing," Jack said. "He just takes what he wants. See, as long as nobody was on it, he just called it his. When the last people who had it died, the heirs put it up for sale without going to *El Patron.*"

"What about this magic spring?" Ted asked.

"Oh, maybe it dried up years ago. Anyway, nobody can find it. But me? I think the reason it dried up is that nobody believes in it anymore," Pablo said.

"Maybe it's hiding from *El Patron,*" Dell suggested.

Pablo nodded. "That could be true. I'll bet it doesn't work for people who do the bad things like *El Patron* does."

Ted snorted. "If that were true, Pablo, we fellows in the white hats would be out of a job."

"That still doesn't explain why he didn't buy the ranch if he wants to keep others off it," Dell said.

"Pablo's right about one thing. *El Patron* thinks he owns it anyway," Chance said quietly. "Just like he thinks he owns the whole county."

"He practically does. And if somebody bucks him, they just disappear," Jack said bitterly. "Look at poor old Jorge. His wife, Lucinda, is going crazy worrying about him. Cora spent the afternoon with her yesterday, and she says Lucinda's sure *El Patron* did something to him. All because he wouldn't sell him that strip of land along the river.''

"Yeah. Poor little thing. And we can't find a thing to prove *El Patron* had a damn thing to do with his vanishing,'' Ted corroborated. "He always has half a dozen of his henchmen doing his dirty work, so we can't pin a thing on him. Hell, they don't even mind going to prison for him.''

"Of course not,'' Jack said. "He picks up the tab for their whole family while they sit in jail. You know, I heard he even sends some of their kids to college? How do you like that? Whack a guy and get your kid's tuition free. It's the new college savings plan.''

Chance allowed the swell of outrage to continue for a few minutes, then raised his hand. "That's it exactly. *El Patron* operates as if the laws of this country don't apply to him whatsoever. Yet he manages to hide from us behind a stone wall of attorneys. He doesn't even screw up on his taxes. We know he's behind it all, but even after six months of intense investigation, we've still got zip in the way of actual proof on the guy. As to this Rancho Milagro? To his way of thinking, why should he pay money for something that he can have for the simple taking?''

His friends nodded soberly.

"Those women at the ranch…they're really hiring? Cowboys?'' Jack said it as if it were a four-letter word.

"Cowboys,'' Chance affirmed. "In addition to everything else, they're missing two hundred some odd head of cattle.''

Ted whistled again. "Those the ones *El Patron*'s

chief boy, Rudy, boasted of finding a month or so back?"

"It wouldn't surprise me to find the brands have been modified," Chance said placidly. He reached for his hat.

Jack sighed. "I suppose you want us to go and get them back."

"No," Chance said, dusting off his sleeves from the morning's accumulated dry sand silt that blew in and settled on his desk when the August winds blew from the west. "Not yet. First, I want Pablo and I to go be cowboys for a while."

As one, the group gaped at him. Dell finally chuckled. "You're always out there, Chance, thinking up the next joke. We walk right into them every time."

"No joke this time. The people who bought this ranch are women from back East. They have more dreams than knowledge and more money than sense. In essence, boys, they don't have the slightest notion of up or down in these parts. Personally, I don't think it's very neighborly of us to let *El Patron* run roughshod over them. So Pablo and I are going to hire on as cowboys."

"And catch *El Patron* red-handed in the bargain?"

"If it's him, I'd call that pretty fine icing on the cake, wouldn't you?" Chance asked.

"You kidding? I've got a sweet tooth for nailing this guy."

"What's going to make them hire you? I'll bet between the four of us—five, Pablo, sorry—we couldn't figure out how to rope a cow, let alone how to drive one."

"Me? I know cows," Pablo said hotly. "My uncle,

he has lots of cattle on his ranch. Branding, cutting, butchering, you name it, I've done it all.''

"See?" Chance asked. "We're already a step ahead of the game.''

"But how are you gonna be the ones the women hire?" Jack asked again.

"Yeah, and even if they did hire you—which I doubt big time—how are you going to hide from *El Patron* out there? I can't even get insurance on my car because he's always got some flunky tearing mine up. One time it was keying the paint job, another time it was a broken windshield. Random vandalism, my good hat. The insurance companies want proof. I'd love to give them proof, all right.'' Ted growled. "Fact is, *El Patron* eats us Feds for an after siesta snack, man. The only ones he doesn't bother are you and Pablo. You, because he doesn't even know you *are* a Fed, just some has-been rodeo jockey, and Pablo because he's related to half the blamed county.''

"We could call my uncle," Pablo suggested, as he often did when *El Patron* was mentioned. This particular uncle was spending fifteen years in the state penitentiary for having tried to kill *El Patron* several years before, following his discovery that the man had arranged the burning of his ranch and home and the slaughter of his animals. Pablo never seemed to find the fact that his uncle had not succeeded and was incarcerated for his failure a particular drawback to his suggestion.

"You've always got some uncle," Dell muttered.

"Fourteen of them," Pablo said proudly. "On my father's side. No relation to the boss, here.''

"Any of them related to *El Patron?*" Ted asked, and Chance could see he was immediately sorry when

Pablo sprang to his feet. Suddenly the little man didn't seem nearly so small. The team's man Friday abruptly became a badger, short, feisty and able to take on a grizzly.

Ted raised both hands, surrendering. "No offense meant, man. I was just hoping. Because then we could round up your cousins, sisters, aunts, uncles—what are there, seven thousand or so of you?—and we could take him out. Not legal, for sure, but one heck of a ride."

Chance cleared his throat, and the tension eased a notch. "I have a plan," he said quietly. "As you pointed out a minute ago, *El Patron* isn't after Pablo because he sees Pablo as a simple hired hand around here—no badge. Everybody knows he's been working here lately, but he's worked a hundred other jobs over the years."

"And you're the rodeo king," Ted said slowly. "The guy who only cadges coffee over at the marshal's office on his daily rounds of mooching lunches, drinks, dinners—and nighttime invitations from pretty ladies."

"Right. That's all anyone knows around here. So no one will be surprised if I go looking for a job to tide me over between rodeo accidents."

"The undercover federal marshal going deeper undercover." Jack groaned. "Just remember, I'm supposed to retire in a few weeks. Don't do anything to screw that up."

"I won't," Chance said.

"Hell, you made me age twenty years the day you pulled back into town a few months ago acting the rodeo circuit cowboy. You even had me fooled for a while. Finally you flashed your badge at me that night. We'd been asking for someone to do something about

El Patron for so long, we never guessed a federal marshal would show up.''

''You're the one who suggested someone come in undercover,'' Chance reminded his senior deputy.

''Well, yeah, but you... I never expected them to send a local guy.''

''It's worked, hasn't it?''

Jack shook his head. ''Yeah, but why make me the supposed marshal? I was doing just fine as a deputy.''

''Paperwork always leaves a trail somewhere,'' Chance said. ''I could change the name on the documents but I couldn't hide the transfer altogether. I may be the most noble of this bunch, but I still like a paycheck now and again.''

His men chuckled.

Jack said, ''I'll tell you, Cora about had a heart attack when I told her I was taking on the title of marshal. She was sure one of *El Patron*'s boys would come gunning for me.''

''An under undercover,'' Ted quipped. ''And I suppose we're supposed to cover you?''

The team moaned at the pun, and Chance said, ''Something like that.''

''But I still don't see why they would hire you and Pablo over somebody with real experience.''

Chance put on his hat and opened the office door. ''What do you think that trophy on my mantel is for, anyway?''

''That tin-plate guy riding a bronco? I thought you got that at a garage sale for fifty cents.''

''Okay, José, can you draw me a picture of a cowboy?'' Jeannie asked, holding out a black crayon to the little boy. She decided she had cowboys on the brain.

Dulce snorted. "Draw? He can't even talk."

Jeannie didn't look at the derisive girl. She was secretly pleased that Dulce had spoken a phrase that didn't contain a swear word.

"Everybody can draw," Jeannie said, then amended, "well, maybe not me."

José gave her a questioning look and slid the blank paper on the butcher-block dining table her way. He pushed her hand, with the crayon still in it, toward the sheet of paper.

Dulce snorted again as Jeannie assumed a look of tremulous courage and bent over the paper. With mock intensity, she drew the worst stick-figure rendition of a cowboy she could conjure. It wore a hat more closely resembling a lumpy pancake than any sort of headgear, boots that could have fit a woolly mammoth, a bandanna roughly the size and shape of Texas and a smile that looked like a jack-o'-lantern's toothy grin.

The drawing certainly didn't appear a thing like the cowboy that had been haunting her dreams the last few nights, the man-wall who grinned at her from every corner of her sleep.

She sighed and assumed a doleful expression as she turned the drawing around for the children to critique. The reaction was all she could have hoped for and more. José giggled behind his short fingers, and even Dulce swiftly hid a bark of laughter.

"You call that a cowboy? Sheesh." Dulce reached for a blank sheet of paper and pulled the crayon from Jeannie's fingers. She started to sketch, then looked up to glare at José and Jeannie. "Did I tell you to watch me?"

Jeannie turned to José. "I heard her say that, didn't

you? She was down on her knees begging us to watch. I thought she'd never stop. 'Please, please watch me.' ''

Dulce snorted, and Jeannie could see the girl clamping her lips tightly together, squeezing back a wayward smile.

Within seconds, the girl tossed the paper across the table and flipped the crayon beside it.

Jeannie realized she'd been holding her breath, half afraid Dulce was going to draw something inappropriate. Instead, she'd lightly executed a shadowy figure on a mesa, thunderclouds in the distance and a long dust coat snared by the wind.

While it was no perfect rendition and was somewhat stiff in form, it was still a remarkable drawing. Jeannie bent closer to José and pulled the sketch so it rested on the table between them. ''Now that's a cowboy. Wow.'' She didn't trust herself to look at the too-silent Dulce. She could feel the girl's fragility like a palpable presence. ''Okay, that settles it.''

''Settles what?'' Dulce asked finally.

''We need an art gallery.'' When José looked a question at her, she explained, ''A place to hang really good pictures.''

José pointed at the blank wall on the south side of the dining room. Jeannie studied it for a moment. ''I think that's perfect. And we have our first one.''

Still without looking at Dulce, she rose from the table and rummaged through a drawer in the sideboard—a sideboard designed to house food and utensils for some twenty children but holding a host of other things, as well—and found some masking tape. A few seconds later, the lonely cowboy drawing was displayed dead center in the middle of the wall.

She stood on the other side of the dining table to

study the effect. The drawing was really quite good but looked too small all alone on the wall. José seemed to think the same thing, for he handed her the atrocious stick figure and pointed at the wall.

She chuckled and shook her head. "Nope, only good drawings for this wall." She waited for Dulce to say something, and when the girl remained silent, she finally risked sneaking a look in her direction. "What do you think?" Jeannie asked softly.

It could have been the light, or perhaps some of the girl's heavy makeup had suddenly dropped into her eyes, but Jeannie could see a definite sheen of tears. They hung in the teenager's eyes for a moment, making the heavy mascara glisten then streak down her cheeks.

"I think it's dumb," she growled and stomped from the room, the sound of her combat boots echoing throughout the house.

Jeannie sighed, feeling a hopeless sense of disconnection with the girl. She couldn't help but wonder if her daughter, Angela ever would have gone through such a phase. Her daughter had been a sunny, happy baby and a sunnier toddler. Surely, Angela would never have grown resentful, nasty and so prickly that even compliments would make her angry and defensive. But then, Angela would never have been abandoned by her parents, wouldn't have been shuffled from one foster-care situation to another, each one seemingly worse than the last.

And perhaps Jeannie couldn't imagine Angela ever being like Dulce because Angela would forever be two years old, chubby-cheeked and cherub-mouthed, giggling at everything from butterflies to tummy tickles. She couldn't imagine it because Angela would never see fifteen, would always and forever be that baby of two years old. Quick, hot tears stung her eyes. The tears were as much from discouragement over Dulce as from the ever sharp pain of Angela's loss.

She felt a feather-soft touch on her hand and blinked away her tears. She had thought perhaps José touched her from sympathy, but he wasn't looking at her. His eyes were locked on the panes of the French doors leading to the broad veranda. He lifted a finger and pointed at the horizon.

Watery from her tears and the afternoon heat, the horizon shimmered in wavy lines against the stark blue sky. A wisp of smoke drifted across the image.

Jeannie's tears dried as suddenly as they'd come, and she dashed to the doors and threw them open. The acrid tang of burning weeds and scorched earth stung her eyes and nose. Sounds carried long distances in the desert, and so did the smell of smoke. And where there was smoke...

She pushed José into the hacienda, telling him to go get Dulce and for both of them to find the housekeeper, Juanita, and stay inside. Jeannie watched him run out of the living room, then slammed the doors behind her and ran for the barn, yelling for Juanita's husband, Tomás.

As Jeannie was finding common on such a large ranch, the man was nowhere to be found. After hurriedly throwing some blankets, a fire extinguisher and two bags of sand into the back of the Jeep, as instructed by the local volunteer fire department after the last range fire, Jeannie tore out of the ranch headquarters.

She tried telling herself the fire wasn't on the headquarters side of the newly created fire wall, but the farther down the road she went, the less hope she had that this was true. The smoke began to obscure the road in places, and the sky became a sickly gray-brown. When the smoke started filtering in the vent system of the Jeep, Jeannie shifted into four-wheel drive and whipped the vehicle into the shallow bar ditch and out, onto the open prairie and away from the smoke.

She proceeded more swiftly than caution dictated, especially given the recent flash-flood type of rains that had created gullies and arroyos where none had existed before. But thanks to the high heat of the past few days, the ground was crusty, and few patches of mud impeded her progress.

Within what seemed like seconds, the sky turned a hot orange-red, and she could see the flames beneath the acrid plumes of smoke. She'd read accounts of fires that wiped out thousands of acres in a matter of minutes. This one was still relatively small, only a couple of hundred feet square. Small enough to contain, she hoped, but large enough to be a very real danger should the wind change direction by the slightest degree.

On the headquarters side of the fire, an old scabrous pickup truck sat cantilevered against a rise, and she could make out two figures rushing in and out of the smoke.

She slammed on the brakes and spun crazily in the sand for a moment or two, killing the Jeep's engine in pure panic. She leaped from the still rocking vehicle, yelling as loudly as possible as she yanked the shovel from the back of the Jeep.

She couldn't recount later what she screamed at the two men before the fire—demands they get off her ranch, commands to put out the fire, threats? All she was cognizant of was a painful, sick fury that someone was harassing her ranch. She hadn't been able to save her husband and daughter from their deaths in that dreadful car accident, but she would stop these creeps who were harming the safe haven she was trying to create for Dulce and little José. She would take them out if she could.

She tore across the expanse of baking desert at hyper speed, pummeling into the most incredible heat she'd ever felt. She'd heard fires likened to living creatures and knew as the smoke-laden air enveloped her that this description was accurate. The flaming beast on her ranch writhed and groaned like a supernatural animal giving birth to hell itself. The blaze didn't crackle or snap like a simple fireplace flame but roared and shrieked, deafening her.

The two men hadn't heard her cries nor, apparently, had they seen her furious approach. They continued fanning the flames with blankets and dancing before the fire as if in glee.

Despite the heat and smoke scorching her lungs, Jeannie managed another almost inhuman cry of rage and hefted the shovel above her shoulder, holding it as if she were a baseball player with a surefire homer coming her way. She aimed directly at one of the men's backs.

The taller of the two men turned toward her as she swung the shovel with all her might. The split second before it connected with his body, Jeannie recognized him and felt a jolt of adrenaline sweep through her. She tried to deflect her vicious swing.

With lightning quick reflexes, Chance Salazar whipped out a hand to catch the handle of the shovel. The impact of the shovel handle against his hand had to hurt, but he gave her a swift, white grin and yanked the shovel from her suddenly limp hands. He flipped the tool like a baton and caught it, then crammed it deep into the ground. With a primal cry, he hauled the combined dirt and sand from the ground and hurled it onto the nearest pocket of flames.

"We have to dig a trench around this section," he yelled. "Wind's blowing toward the road—that's good. If we can block it on this side, it'll likely burn itself out."

The smaller man continued beating at the flames with a blanket, not fanning the fire or dancing in glee as she'd thought, but desperately attempting to smother the rapidly spreading blaze while staying out of its grasp.

She found herself muttering, "Sorry, sorry," as she ran to the Jeep. After snaring the fire extinguisher, she chanted, "Thank you, thank you," on the way back.

As if trained to work as a team, Jeannie and the two men fought side by side to subdue the fiery beast on her ranch. She took the left flank, spraying the ground with the foamy chemical compound. Chance dug a trench and hurtled sand and dirt over the blaze while his friend beat the flames back with the scorched blanket.

It seemed like days before the beast of fire was contained within the confines of the main ranch road and the new trench they'd created. Though empty, the fire extinguisher suddenly seemed to gain fifty pounds in weight, and Jeannie let it slip from her arms and thud to the ground. She stared at the still smoldering desert without comprehension.

Small wisps of smoke rose from patches of twisted and charred plant life, but the westerly wind picked up and began carrying the smoke away, leaving patches of blue sky. Soon the only heat came from the August afternoon sun, hot and blazing but clean.

She felt strangely renewed, powerful. She looked at the two men who had struggled at her side. Soot and sweat streaked their faces. Because they had squinted during the fight, their eyes, though red from the burning weeds, stood out on their dirty faces as if they'd worn goggles. Both men were grinning, and Jeannie knew they were experiencing the same exhilaration she felt.

She looked at the charred land, a large square of black, and scarcely started when Chance Salazar dropped a filthy hand on her shoulder. As she'd done in front of the theater in town, she allowed him to propel her, this time to face him.

"Are you okay?" he asked.

She realized that her unconscious mind had remembered his voice exactly, for this was the corduroy baritone she'd heard in her every dream the past few nights. She nodded.

"Are you sure?"

"Truthfully? I feel great," she said and realized they weren't shouting for the first time in what seemed like hours. "How about you?"

His eyes raked her face, and for half a second Jeannie had the oddest notion that he might kiss her. His hand tightened on her shoulder, and she found herself fighting an urge to lean into him. The natural sounds of the desert—the shriek of a hawk, the rustle of dry grass—were muted to a low thrum that seemed more inside her than out.

Chance smiled. "We're fine."

"I thought—" she started, then broke off, suddenly aware of her surroundings, abruptly aware she'd been about to say she thought he was going to kiss her.

Chance grinned. "I know what you thought."

She could only hope he didn't and that he would attribute her high color to the fire and the baking heat from the sun.

"You thought we started it. You damn near got me with that shovel."

She couldn't help but smile in return, albeit ruefully. "You put it to much better use," she said shakily.

"Well, I think so. You seemed pretty intent on re-arranging my features. And I rather like my face the way it is."

So did she, she thought. Soot and all.

As if reading her mind, he chuckled and shook his head. "Of course, there are plenty of folk who would disagree with me if they could see me now." His friend gave a bark of laughter, and as if only then realizing he was still touching her, Chance dropped his hand from her shoulder.

"You were a godsend," she said simply.

"Thanks." He wanted to say a lot more but couldn't. He wanted to tell her she was in danger and that he was there to help her with her troubles. But he couldn't tell her that, either.

"It wasn't lightning, was it?" she asked, as if resigned to a negative answer.

He gave a ragged chuckle at her recognizing the obvious, relieved she leaped to the truth without him having to tell her and, by telling her, possibly blow his cover. "Whoever started this little fire was long gone by the time we came along."

She looked up, as though she could divine truth from the puffs of lingering smoke, the cloudless blue sky. "So you think it was started deliberately?"

Should he frighten her or not? He didn't know much about her, but he knew she was no fool. A bit out of her element, maybe, and somewhat confused, but there was nothing wrong with her brain cells. She thought something was amiss on her property and now she'd found out she was right. She'd gone to Nando. She'd tried to get help. And, unfortunately for her, Nando had been typically Nando, lazy and fatly paid by *El Patron*.

Instead of trying to duck the issue, Chance said, "Sure. Someone's lighting fires on your place." Damn that Nando Gallegos. How dare he let this lady live in fear?

Pablo asked in Spanish, "Ask her if she knows how much *El Patron* is paying the sheriff."

Chance ignored his cousin. He pointed to the near perfect square shape. "Somebody poured gas around the edges, tossed and match and let the wind do the rest. Lightning usually sparks a patch and builds out. And trust me, you'd hear it hit the ground. And except for the occasional heat lightning, you generally need a few clouds around before you have lightning." He looked at the utterly clear sky, then at the blackened earth. "You have a solid square here. Looks very deliberate to me."

He jerked his head toward the ranch road. "Saw a couple of other patches like this on the way in. Somebody's been giving you a pretty hard time, haven't they?"

She felt as if a tremendous weight had been removed from her shoulders. "No one's been hurt," she said.

"Except the grassland. And your nerves."

She gave a half shrug. Now that someone else had seen the damage and believed her, she discovered her nerves weren't nearly so frayed. "What are you doing

out here?'' She added hurriedly, ''Not that I'm object-
ing, of course.''

He looked almost embarrassed and exchanged a look
with his friend, who suddenly busied himself dusting
off his worn jeans.

''It's good you don't object, because the thing is
we're here about that job for the cowhands.''

''Cowhands?'' she asked blankly.

The smaller man said something in Spanish, and
Chance gave a brief chuckle. ''Cowboys,'' he corrected. ''We came to apply for the job.'' He waved his
friend over. ''This is Pablo Garcia. He's a distant
cousin of mine.''

''You're applying for the job?'' she asked. She'd
wanted him to apply. She'd dreamed of him applying.
But because she'd leaned into his touch, because she'd
thought he was going to kiss her, she didn't know what
to think. His working for her wasn't in the picture, was
it?

''Between us, we've got all the experience you
need.''

''But—'' Jeannie suddenly didn't know why she was
arguing. He and his friend had proven invaluable in an
emergency. His being there was one of the ranch's miracles, not a problem.

''I don't want to be pushy, ma'am—''

She smiled at him, ''I hear a but coming.''

He grinned. ''But I'm pretty sure you could do a lot
worse than us.''

Almost as if in answer to this statement, they heard
the sound of two car horns honking from the main
ranch road. Four men poured out of each dusty vehicle
and swiftly made their way across the rough terrain.

"*Carámba,*" Chance's cousin Pablo muttered, stiffening.

Jeannie was aware that Chance had tensed, as well.

When the eight men were within hailing distance, one of them called, "Señora McMunn? You having some trouble?"

She was surprised they knew her name. She'd never seen them before, that she knew of.

The man who had called slapped his chest. "I'm Rudy Martinez. Nando Gallegos sent us out here. The sheriff? He said you talked with him? You're expecting us, no?"

Before she could stammer an answer, Chance stepped in front of her. "Sorry, Rudy, but the lady's already hired out."

Jeannie blinked at his falsehood, though she couldn't help but smile at his sheer audacity and was glad his broad back hid her grin from the sheriff's boys. She stepped from behind Chance and somehow wasn't surprised that he sidestepped again, as if providing a shield for her with his body.

Instead of looking chagrined or disappointed, the spokesman for the eight men laughed. "She hired you and Pablo? Didn't know she was throwing a rodeo for ladies' men and errand boys."

Pablo muttered something under his breath and started forward, only to subside at a single hand gesture from Chance.

Rudy stepped to the side, not in any fear of Pablo, but apparently so he could talk directly to Jeannie. His grin still covered his swarthy face. "Since I promised my cousin I'd keep an eye out for you, I'll come back in a couple of days. If you've changed your mind and want to hire some real men, you can tell me then. Until then, *señora*, I'd lock my doors both day and night.''

He signaled the remaining seven, and almost as one they turned. About halfway across the field, they broke into laughter and looked back, only to laugh all the harder.

Pablo spat on the ground in overt defiance of their hilarity.

Chance turned and met Jeannie's eyes. ''So…do we have the job?''

''Those were the sheriff's men,'' she said.

Chance looked from her to the retreating cars. ''Right,'' he said, and met her eyes. ''So do we have the job?'' he repeated, grinning at her.

Jeannie could only stare at him, half admiring his brazen disregard of the ordinary conventions and half appalled at herself for this admiration.

Pablo said something in Spanish, and Chance's grin broadened. ''Pablo wants to know what kind of horses you're offering us.''

''I don't—I mean, we don't have any yet. I was…'' She trailed off, realizing she was as much as admitting they had the job as she was apologizing for not having the horses as yet.

''No problem,'' Chance said, picking up the shovel and the empty fire extinguisher and tossing them to Pablo, who caught them with a laugh. ''We'll hit the next horse auction in Carlsbad or maybe up in Roswell, and we'll help you pick out a couple of good ones.'' He took her arm and began leading her to their vehicles.

Pablo said something, and again Chance translated. ''He says he hopes dinner's pretty soon, he's nearly starving.''

Jeannie stopped in her tracks and stared at the two men.

"What's wrong?" Chance asked, and then grinned as if he knew exactly what was troubling her. Pablo grinned, too.

"Nothing," Jeannie said, resuming her pace and smiling broadly. She knew it was crazy and that her friends Leeza and Corrie would probably never stop kidding her for her impulsiveness and that she'd probably just made an enemy of the local sheriff, but she hadn't felt so good in ages. "Nothing's wrong at all. I was just thinking that for the first time in a long time, I simply can't wait for dinner."

Chapter 4

Contrary to Jeannie's orders, José and Dulce stood waiting for them on the front veranda of the main house. The protective anger in Dulce's eyes—and the wide-eyed fear in José's—quelled any remonstrance Jeannie might have uttered.

"It's all right," she said, jumping out of the Jeep. She signaled to Chance that he should wait a minute while she got the key to the bunkhouse. She reached out and ruffled José's straight black mop of hair and lightly touched Dulce on the shoulder. While José leaned into her touch, Dulce shrugged away from it.

José pointed to Chance's pickup.

"Who are those weirdos?" Dulce asked as if translating. She lifted her chin at the two men in the truck.

Jeannie gave her a repressive look then said, "They're two men who helped me put out another fire. I've just hired them to help out with things here at the ranch." She felt almost dazed by the admission. She'd hired two strangers as cowboys for her ranch. Was she crazy?

"Things like us kids? I knew all this lovey-dovey stuff wouldn't last very long."

Jeannie felt her breath hitch. *Lovey-dovey stuff?* She'd been walking on proverbial eggshells around the two of them. The most she'd done was touch a cheek or pat a shoulder. If the girl considered that lovey-dovey, she'd probably expire on the spot from a real hug.

"No," Jeannie said as breezily as she could manage through her constricted throat, "they're here to take care of things like cattle, fences and range fires. I expect everyone on this ranch to treat these men with respect. Is that clear?"

José nodded, his eyes solemn. Dulce snorted. "I give as good as I get. They treat me right, I'll think about doing the same. Otherwise, screw 'em."

"They're going to help us get some horses," Jeannie said. She hoped her tone was light. She brushed past the girl to the rack of keys just inside the front doors.

She was halfway back to the Jeep when she heard Dulce call. "Are you gonna let us kids ride horses, too?"

Jeannie turned in time to catch a look of intense longing on Dulce's features, possibly the first genuine sign of girlhood she'd seen on that painted face. "Of course," she said, grinning. "This is a ranch, isn't it?"

Dulce hitched a shoulder, turned away without another word and stomped inside the house.

Jeannie fought the urge to call the girl back. When she'd found the advertisement for this broken-down ranch in southeastern New Mexico, she'd dreamed she could create a happy home for troubled children. She'd pictured herself—and her two friends—playing sweet home mothers to countless children who needed them.

She hadn't taken the children themselves into account. Or reality.

From the moment the two children had arrived at Rancho Milagro, she'd begun to slam face first into her misconceptions. José couldn't be sweeter, however noncommunicative, but Dulce was a walking world of pain.

As she did every time the girl grated on her nerves, Jeannie tried telling herself that what had been destroyed in Dulce's life with harsh words and scowls could be built up with laughter and a caring touch. She'd dared to hope that was true. But she was afraid that too many years of anger and distrust had left an indelible mark on the prickly child.

She lifted her hand in a wave to José and signaled him to wait for her. He waggled little fingers at her and gave a tiny smile, and Jeannie realized that while she might have mountains yet to climb with the queen of recalcitrance, José was a total mystery but a darling one. And at least Dulce was curious enough to ask about horses.

Jeannie felt a sudden wave of hopefulness sweep over her. She didn't know if the hope's source lay in the small toehold of rapport with the children. Was it a residue of the fire's adrenaline rush? Or could it be laid at the feet of Chance Salazar, who once again was waiting patiently for her?

She found herself abruptly confident. She hopped into the Jeep Cherokee and pulled forward, motioning for Chance to follow her.

Moments later, she stopped in front of the long, low-slung bunkhouse. The building had once been a crumbling adobe barn, but Jeannie and her partners had designated it quarters for a few of the teachers or ranch hands they might eventually need. It sported eight separate bedrooms, smallish to be sure, but perfectly adequate, and two large communal-style shower rooms and bathrooms—his and hers. The living quarters were spacious, with four separate sofas, a few comfortable chairs, a large television and VCR combination and a stereo, none of which were new, but all were attractive and functional. The living room and dining room were under the same beamed high ceiling, which they had elevated to add a clerestory window, and the kitchen would easily accommodate five industrious chefs using the utensils and flatware stacked neatly in the open cabinets.

Except for the myriad inspectors and the contractors, Chance and Pablo were the first two strangers to see the results of her efforts at Rancho Milagro. Jeannie found herself showing the bunkhouse as if to prospective buyers, and their very silence added to her pride.

She risked a glance at Chance and found she couldn't read his expression. His eyes were on a Holly Huber print hanging on one of the bedroom walls. It was of a bucking horse, bent nearly double in his defiance, flying mane and tail in raging motion. While the painting was comprised only of sketch lines and a vivid green color wash, the overall effect was one of sheer power and raw anger.

"That horse reminds me of the girl back at the main house," Chance said. "All sound and fury."

Jeannie gazed at the print as if for the first time. He was right. The similarities between the girl and the horse were subtle but deep—wild things, refusing any and all attempts at taming. She wondered if knowing such a thing would help her with the girl. She surmised that if Dulce suspected Jeannie thought such a thing, the girl would hate her all the more for seeing through her defenses.

Chance found his breath catching as the soot-streaked redhead beside him studied the painting on the wall of the elegant bunkhouse. She looked for all the world as if she was analyzing the print for proof of his statement. He'd never had someone take his words so to heart before.

She frowned and then sighed. He could read her emotions as easily as a first-grade primer. Just as her comments in her notepad jumped from subject to subject, her every emotion seemed to flit across her features—curiosity, determination, fear, hope. Every nuance of what she felt seemed to leap to the soft curves of her lovely freckled Irish face.

"I wouldn't want to tame her," she murmured. "I think enough people have tried doing that to her that she's wild out of sheer last resort."

"There's breaking and there's gentling," he said.

She turned to him, and he wished he hadn't spoken, for her eyes were luminous and too blue. He had the strangest image of a child they might jointly produce, one with dark red hair and blue-green eyes.

A soft smile curved her lips, and he suddenly wanted to touch them, to run a finger across her cheek, as much to see if she felt like the freckled peach she resembled as to wipe away a smudge of soot.

Her lips parted slightly, and he found himself leaning forward, as though her mouth had become a magnet that could command his entire body.

"I'm glad you're here," she said, and her eyes let him know this was nothing short of the absolute truth.

Her words, the simplicity of them and the almost dreamy expression on her face—not to mention the outrageous image he'd conjured of their child—served as a glass of icy water tossed directly into his face. He tended to run with women who had been around more than a couple of blocks. They generally sported short skirts, big hair and no tears the morning after. They seldom spoke of feelings beyond like or dislike of the latest country and western tune and would never have revealed their shellacked hearts by uttering such a disarming statement.

He edged back a step and found himself struggling not to shuffle his feet. "Yeah, me, too," he muttered, lying through his teeth.

This had been a damn fool idea. He'd thought he could play the hero, rescue the girl, vanquish the bad guy and ride off into the sunset unscathed and undiscovered. Riding the rodeo circuit and as a federal marshal, he'd made a career of rushing in to save the day and disappearing as quickly. He'd never had to reckon with a red-haired siren who wore her vulnerability on her skin.

As if she could see right into him, she smiled gently and laid her hand on his crossed arms. "Thank you, Chance."

His mama had taught him to say you're welcome when thanks were offered, but manners were the furthest thing from his head. And saying you're welcome would somehow imply much more than it should.

She released his arm, and he felt as if he could breathe again. She turned to the door. "I'm assuming you need to go back to town for your things...."

"No, ma'am," he said and, with her safely some ten feet away, felt his confidence return. He grinned at her, somewhat enjoying the turning of the tables. She'd made him feel as off balance as a man could feel. It was only fair he do the same to her. "We brought our stuff with us. Just in case."

"Oh." She frowned, then seemed to shrug whatever she was thinking away. "That's good. I suppose you'll want to clean up before dinner. Juanita usually serves it around six." She smiled and lifted a hand in farewell. "See you both then."

As soon as the door of the bunkhouse—which was far more like a real house than either he or Pablo had seen in a host of years—closed, Pablo said, "You gonna tell her, boss?"

"Tell her what?" Chance asked, going to the window to watch her drive to the main hacienda. When she'd disappeared from view, he found his eyes focusing on the freshly painted wall of another of her outbuildings. She'd made a beautiful job of the restorations. Everything about the place subtly suggested peace and tranquillity. He found himself more determined than ever to outsmart *El Patron*—if he was indeed the source of her harassment.

"You gonna tell her that you're really a marshal?"

Chance sighed. If she were anyone else, he wouldn't give the notion a second thought. Both in business and in his personal life, he operated strictly on a need-to-know basis. "I can't think of a single good reason for doing so," he said finally.

"I can," Pablo said.

"Name one."

"She's nice. And she's smart, too."

''Okay, she's nice and she's smart. Those aren't reasons for telling her we're undercover here.''

''She's not the kind of woman you play games with.''

''I'm not going to play games with her. I'm just going to make sure *El Patron* doesn't mess with her ranch.''

''And if we don't catch him soon?''

''What are you saying, Pablo?''

''How long are we gonna stay? A week? Two? Six months?''

''As long as it takes.''

''Okay, boss.''

''I mean it, Pablo. There's no reason to tell her anything. We're here now, and that's all there is to it.''

''Okay, boss.''

''I'm not out to date the lady, much less hurt her. I'm here to do a job. Nothing more.''

''Okay, boss.''

''Cut it out, will you?''

''Didn't you tell me she had a housekeeper and her husband working here?''

''Yeah. Doreen said they're a couple that used to work at Job Corps in Roswell. Originally from Mexico.''

''Where were they when the fire started, do you think?''

Chance looked at his friend and distant cousin and smiled. ''That's a very good question, Pablo. Why don't we get cleaned up and go find out?''

Chance wasn't sure what he'd expected the main house to look like, perhaps a cross between the front cover of a modern design magazine and southwest corny. Instead, the immediate impression the house gave was one of rich harmony of textures, earth colors and warmth.

Burned-red Saltillo tile graced the entryway and ran the length of the expansive living room. Thick, plush, handwoven carpets broke up the austerity in front of sofas, small sitting arrangements and the large kiva-style fireplace. The Taos furniture with its pine arms and legs and lush, overstuffed cushions of brown brushed leather complemented the exquisite landscapes and wooden artifacts on the living room walls.

The flanking dining room seemed an extension of the main room, a huge pine planked table taking up the center of the room with enough chairs around it to seat an army. A matching sideboard was the only adornment to the wall except for a smallish drawing taped over the sideboard.

The little boy who had been on the front porch earlier let them in and gave both of them a shy smile before gesturing them into the dining room. He dashed around the massive table and pointed at the drawing on the wall.

Chance and Pablo walked closer and peered across the table at the sketch.

"Did you draw that?" Chance asked.

The boy shook his head emphatically. He screwed up his face to a mean scowl and pinched the side of his nose.

Chance had to chuckle. The boy had pantomimed the wildly dressed and painted girl to near perfection. He wondered if the boy was deaf as well as mute. He obviously understood English so he could at least read lips. He grinned at the boy. "Ah, that girl did."

A voice behind him said, "That girl's name is Miss Quiñones to you, cowboy."

He turned to find the girl inside the archway to the dining room, her wildly painted face set and hard, her eyes glittering with challenge.

"Well, Miss Quiñones to you, you certainly can draw."

She gave him a suspicious look. "Like you know anything about art."

Chance decided valor called for not replying to that gambit. He picked up the drawing on the table. It was the worst drawing he'd ever seen, and it was hard not to smile. "This is interesting," he said politely. "Yours?" he asked the boy.

The boy giggled softly and shook his head. He pointed at the girl.

"Puh-lease!" The girl made gagging sounds. Her eyes brightened in amusement as Jeannie came in from the swinging kitchen door and stopped in seeming shock. "It's *hers*."

Chance felt as though a lung decided to stop working. His breath caught and warred for escape from his chest. He'd seen her on the sunny Carlsbad street, curly red hair pulled in a ponytail, neat and trim as picture from an L.L. Bean catalog. He'd seen her furiously hefting a shovel straight for his head, her eyes filled with murder. He'd seen her bedraggled and sooty and triumphant. And he'd seen her dewy-eyed soft in the bunkhouse, her hair sweaty and her face smudged and her inner thoughts on her very skin.

The woman standing in the doorway with an exaggerated look of chagrin on her face was another person altogether. She'd showered and changed into a silky summer dress that nearly touched the floor, but that transformation was the least of the differences. This Jeannie had curling tendrils of auburn red hair trailing down the sides of her face, amused, confident eyes fixed on the group of them and such an obvious well of hope for the children, and maybe even Chance and Pablo, that he couldn't begin to think what to say to her.

He was certain the smile she wore was genuine, just as the smile she'd given him earlier had been. But he was equally sure that the smile hid a deep sorrow over something, that her gentle eyes hid a veritable torrent of tears. He didn't think it would take a whole lot to make those tears start to flow, and he told himself that, like most men, he sure didn't want to be around when they did.

"That's my work," Jeannie said, pointing at the ludicrous sketch in his limp grasp. She stepped forward and snatched it, turning away to fold it sloppily and shove it in a drawer in the sideboard.

To his wonder, she gave him the briefest of winks before saying, "We only put the best work on the wall of our new art gallery." She gestured at the single drawing on the sideboard wall. "Dulce's sketch holds the sole place of honor for the moment."

Chance had always thought himself lucky. He'd been born into a fairly wealthy ranching family in the Carlsbad area. As a result of that and good parents, he'd never really had to scrounge for affection or basic needs. He saw what Jeannie was trying to do for Dulce Quiñones to you. In all her life, the girl had probably never been truly recognized, let alone praised.

Jeannie's doing so somehow managed to include not just Dulce, but Pablo, José and Chance. Without a hint of sexual overture, she'd winked at him, drawing him into a family environment, encouraging him to share a rare moment with them. The fact that at that moment she reminded him vaguely of his mother made him acutely uncomfortable.

"Don't you think it's great?" Jeannie asked, prompting him with her adjective.

He turned as if to consider the drawing again. "You've really got a good idea here. An art gallery. And that drawing. It's terrific. You know, Pablo knows how to make frames. What about a frame for it?"

"I think that's a wonderful idea," Jeannie said. Her gaze shifted to Pablo. "I noticed you only spoke in Spanish to Chance before. Do you speak English?"

Chance had to withhold a glance in his cousin's direction when the man blithely said—in Spanish—that he didn't speak a word of English. It was only when Jeannie turned her eyes to his that, out of habit, he translated the negative. The lie. Another lie.

Surprising him, Jeannie didn't talk to him, but turned her clear sky-blue gaze to Pablo as she haltingly said in terrible clipped Spanish that she couldn't speak much of the language but hoped he would be buried at Rancho Milagro.

Chance would have chuckled aloud, but his cousin's reaction choked the laugh right out of him. The little man he would have sworn could never have been courtly in his life nodded solemnly and lifted Jeannie's hand to his lips in as archaic a gesture as Chance had ever seen outside a movie theater and answered her in Spanish. "For you, *señora,* and because my cousin is an imbecile, I would walk through the coals of hell."

Chance edged a little closer to Pablo and managed to press his boot onto Pablo's toe. His cousin never flinched, continued to smile. Through a dry throat,

Chance mistranslated for Pablo, "He hopes so, too."
Pablo pushed him off his foot and gave him a poke in
the ribs. Chance proffered English words. "For you,
señora, he says he'll do anything."

José gave them a curious look, and Dulce's black
lips twitched, but, if they knew the language, neither
of them corrected his translation. Jeannie smiled at
Pablo as if all were well and life was pleasant.

While Chance couldn't figure out why Pablo had
decided their stay at Rancho Milagro might be better
for the marshal to be permanent translator, he'd already
made the plunge and had gone along with the ruse. He
supposed Pablo had decided that people might say
things in front of him that they would withhold if they
thought he spoke English. It was movie logic, Chance
thought, and all too likely to backfire. Pablo obviously
hadn't considered the ramifications of someone—Jeannie, in particular—finding out that he did speak English, and rather well at that. On the one hand, Pablo
was giving him grief to tell Jeannie why they were
really at the ranch, and on the other, he was lying
through his slightly crooked teeth.

"I would pay him for it, of course. Extra, I mean,"
Jeannie said. "Oh, that reminds me…we didn't even
talk about salary earlier."

"Later," Chance said quickly. He gave a glance toward the kids as if they were the reason he felt uncomfortable. The truth was, he couldn't, in all conscience,
take money from this woman when he and Pablo were
being paid fairly well by the federal government—contrary to his friend Jack's complaints. Even if she had
money to burn, it wouldn't be acceptable. He'd have
to come up with some salary, however, as she'd be
suspicious if he refused payment—and *El Patron*

would find about it and immediately smell a rat. The famous layabout Chance Salazar working free? He'd just have to stick her money in some fund for the ranch's later use.

"Right," she said, as if reading his thoughts. "Later. After dinner. Okay. Kiddos, if you'll go into the kitchen, Juanita has the plates and silverware ready to set out on the sideboard, and I think she could probably use some help bringing in the food." As the kids left the room, she turned to Pablo and Chance and said, "I hope you like chicken. Juanita's a marvelous cook as well as the housekeeper. But unfortunately, *pollo* is about the only Spanish word I recognize on her list of possible dinners, so until I learn more, we'll probably be having it often."

"Chicken's great," Chance said. What had possessed the woman to buy a ranch so close to the border if she didn't speak Spanish?

"You hate chicken," Pablo murmured in Spanish. "Too many times mucking the henhouse."

"Oh," Jeannie said, focusing her too-blue eyes on Pablo, "you like chicken, too? That's wonderful."

"Can we do anything to help?" Chance asked to forestall Pablo as much as to take his mind off Jeannie's raw vulnerability. He told himself he was like the housekeeper who proclaimed she wouldn't do windows—he was the marshal who couldn't do vulnerable.

She gave him a piercing look as if she could hear his thoughts, then suggested they wander about the place. "To familiarize yourselves, you know. I think dinner will be about fifteen minutes, so why not just look around?"

She finished her words with a shooing gesture and turned away before he could think of a reply. He re-

alized that by signing on as one of the cowboys she'd
asked for in the paper, and by telling her he rode the
rodeo circuit, he'd inadvertently relegated himself to
the same status as the children she housed on the ranch.
He was someone who needed looking after. The notion
was somewhat daunting.

Watching her disappear into the kitchen and feeling
like an idiot, he turned to Pablo. "What the hell was
all that translation business?"

In Spanish, Pablo said, "I don't know what you're
talking about. And besides which, didn't I recommend
you tell her the truth? If you can lie to her, so can I.
Anyway, I like her Spanish. And you can tell her for
me that I said I hope you're going to be buried here,
too." Pablo cackled.

"You gonna stand here all night cracking wise or
are we gonna check out the place?"

Jeannie thought dinner at Rancho Milagro that night
was a miracle in itself. If pressed to find a word, she'd
have called it a boisterous affair. José remained non-
verbal but giggled often. Dulce stuck to recalcitrance
but showed a knack for one-liners. Pablo remained res-
olutely linguistically challenged, but something he said
made both Dulce and José giggle, letting Jeannie know
for the first time that both of them must speak Spanish.

And then there was Chance.

Chance dominated the table like some roving trou-
badour with tall tales and outrageous feats of glory. He
lowered or raised his scratchy baritone in telling stories
he'd heard, thought or once upon a time dreamed of.
He controlled the assembly like a tent revivalist at a
bilingual Easter Sunday service. They laughed or were

horrified, shocked or satisfied by each and every yarn he spun.

Only Juanita and Tomás didn't hear the stories. As per their preferred agreement, they took their meals separately in the kitchen. And given Juanita's surprise when she saw Pablo and Chance at the table and the narrow look of suspicion—or fear—on the house-keeper's features, Jeannie thought their absence might be for the best.

She didn't know if the secret to the evening lay in the simple fact that she'd been so long without adult companionship. She thought of the times she'd laughed and bonded with her dearest friends Leeza and Corrie and how much they would have enjoyed the stories.

But even with Leeza and Corrie, she hadn't laughed so hard or so freely in the two long years without David and Angela as she did on this rare evening. Maybe some of that came from Chance's ignorance about her circumstances. With Leeza and Corrie, Jeannie always had the feeling they were waiting for her to finally break down. And here was a stranger who knew nothing of David or Angela, didn't know about her tear-stained pillows or the dark moments over the last two years when she'd craved joining her lost family.

Feeling as if she'd been neglecting the children in the rollicky aftermath of the meal, guilty that she could have such a good time in the company of two new cowhands—one of whom didn't even speak English— she looked across the table and saw a sleepy but smil-ing José and an equally tired but reluctant to admit it Dulce. Relieved, she realized the children had enjoyed the company every bit as much as she had.

She wryly tried telling herself that the sole cause for

the enjoyment was novelty. For obvious reasons, she didn't object to being caught out in her own lie.

"Kiddos?" she asked at the first lull in the conversation and long after Juanita's excellent caramel flan— so far she'd been grateful she wasn't able to decipher desserts on Juanita's proposed menus, as every night proved a taste delight—had been removed. "Don't you think it's about time for bed?"

"Give me a break. I'm not a little baby," Dulce said, but pushed her chair back from the table anyway.

To Jeannie's consternation, the girl delivered a slow, would-like-to-be sultry look to Chance, who luckily— or wisely—ignored whatever message the teenager had in mind. After a couple of seconds, Dulce sighed and instead of clomping from the room in a huff, the girl gently nudged José into awareness, hefted him from his chair into a walking position, then held his shoulders as they started to leave the room. She turned at the archway and said, "I'll put him to bed. Okay?"

Jeannie felt as if the world turned sideways on its axis. Her heart skipped a full beat or two. "T-thank you, Dulce. That would be wonderful."

When the children had departed the main living area, surely feeling the adult eyes on their slender backs, she heard Chance say softly, *"You're* wonderful."

She dragged her gaze from the empty hallway to the man across the table from her. "What?"

Their eyes locked. Perhaps it was the wine or the glow from the candles that made his cheeks seem to redden. "You're doing a wonderful thing here," he said, and though she was certain it wasn't what he'd already said, it warmed her nonetheless.

"She's putting José to bed," she said, and felt inane. "Or she might be throwing him in the well for the sheer spite of it,'' he said. But he said it softly and with a smile on his lips.

Jeannie chuckled and shook her head. The fact that she knew it wasn't true was a milestone of major proportions. She'd spent many an uneasy moment wondering just what the angry girl might do.

Pablo said something in Spanish that Chance didn't bother to translate. Chance said something, and the two men laughed with easy camaraderie. Jeannie smiled at the deep rumbling sound. It was odd to discover how much she'd missed the bass notes. Surrounded by the soprano and alto voices of her friends, the descant of the children, she hadn't realized how much richer the world felt with bass harmony.

Sitting at the table with these two men, listening to Chance's outlandish tales and laughing with him and Pablo, she'd felt as though some kind of bizarre magic had infected them all. And, having watched the bristly Dulce perform a true act of unsolicited kindness, she was sure of it.

Somehow, between the chicken and the flan, they'd become a unit of sorts. Not a family in the sense of the strong bonds that only time and commitment could produce, but a cohesive group nevertheless.

Pablo pushed back his chair, hiding a yawn. He blushed and bowed. He begged so many excuses Jeannie couldn't begin to follow his Spanish.

Chance stood up to go, as well, and Jeannie found herself asking him to stay. "We still have to talk about your salaries," she said. And what he thought of the sheriff, the sheriff's men, the children, the fire they'd fought that afternoon, the dream of Rancho Milagro and why he smelled of sunshine and soap after a candlelit dinner.

Yet, when Pablo had made his farewells and she'd checked on the children—José was fast asleep in his bed, Dulce glowering at her from her desk where she was busy drawing—she found she couldn't conjure up the words she wanted to say to Chance. They were strangers, the rodeo cowboy, now her hired hand, and she, the uncertain lady of the hacienda.

They stood on the veranda of the main house. The desert air was redolent with the scent of second-blooming Spanish broom and cool with a soft breeze from the north. In Maryland, outside the city, she was often able to find three or four constellations. Here, in the middle of the black desert, so many stars jeweled the sky she couldn't even pick out the most well known of them. If David had been here, she would have moved to stand in front of him and he would have wrapped his arms around her like a shawl. She would have drawn his warmth to her, basked in his love.

But this wasn't David she stood beside, and she couldn't ask Chance to simply hold her. She needed to say something, if only to show she still could. "I hate to admit this, but I've no idea what to pay you."

"You just say whatever comes into your head, don't you?" he asked.

She was glad of the darkened veranda, for he couldn't see her blush. David had often said the same thing of her. And her friends Leeza and Corrie teased her about her non sequiturs and notebook truths on a constant basis.

"Not always," she said finally. And starkly honestly.

He made the sound that men issue when their minds seem elsewhere, a cross between a grunt and a hum.

"It almost feels like you can see the whole Milky Way from here," she said.

"So beautiful," he murmured.

A shooting star streaked across the sky.

"We can't see those in D.C.," she said. "Except during once-in-a-lifetime meteor storms."

"I'm sorry," he said and, at his next words, she realized he wasn't being sympathetic for her lack. "I wasn't looking at the sky."

His tone, even more than his words, made her all too aware that he'd been staring at her and that, unlike her, he could see clearly in the dark. She looked at her hands, grasping the wooden railing that lined the veranda. They appeared bleached in the starlight, with fingers that belonged to someone else, someone who had loved too dearly once and didn't dare allow that kind of pain in her life again. Yet they ached to lift from the railing to simply touch the man standing beside her in the night. To touch.

She drew a deep breath. "I've never been an employer before, except for household help," she said.

"Looks like you're doing just fine," he said softly, almost as if he exhaled the words. "That was a darn fine dinner, and by the end of it, that thorny kid actually smiled at you."

She gave a grimacy smile she hoped he couldn't discern. The thorny description fit Dulce with uncanny accuracy. Again the contrast between Dulce and Angela flitted across her mind. Angela had never stopped smiling.

She cleared her throat. "Thanks," she said, "but the truth is, I don't know how to go about this. I liked having you—and Pablo, of course—here for dinner. I'd like that to continue, if you don't mind. Breakfast, too.

And I guess we can pack a lunch for you or you can
come in for lunch. And I liked how you handled the
art gallery. And your stories were—''

She had no idea how long she might have continued
babbling had he not stopped her by placing a hand on
her arm. She looked at him in alarm and, she thought
fearfully, an almost wistful longing.

She couldn't read his face. She could barely see him.
But she could feel the heat radiating from his body,
defying the cool desert night breeze.

''I don't start until tomorrow,'' he said, and slid his
hand up her arm and gently pulled her closer to him.
Her head felt light, her mind numb.

''I don't understand,'' she murmured, even as she
leaned unresistingly into his embrace.

''Meaning I can't do this then.'' He lowered his lips
to hers, and unlike she'd anticipated, unlike she'd
known with David, his kiss wasn't sweet and soft, but
demanding and sure. He tasted of wine with a hint of
the caramel flan and sheer, raw desire.

Surprised, she started, but his other hand encircled
her, drawing her closer to him. It was only as he
pressed her tightly against him that she could feel his
increased heart rate and hear his ragged breathing.

Vaguely understanding that whatever prompted him
to kiss her carried nothing idle about it, she moaned
softly. When his lips touched hers a second time, she
sighed into his mouth and melted into his body.

If his heartbeat was hurried, racing, hers was chaotic,
ragged and thready. Feelings so long buried that she'd
thought them gone completely suddenly burst into
flame, swelling from the places he touched to engulf
her and make her weak with want and ache for more.

His kiss deepened, and his hands pulled her roughly

to him as if trying to pull her inside him. And she went willingly, mindlessly into the kiss, into the passion she'd denied for so very long.

An eternity seemed to pass before he lifted his head, and then it only seemed that he'd risen for desperate air, clutching her hair in his hands as if she caused him pain of some kind and holding himself as rigid as the pillars supporting her veranda roof.

She could feel every nuance of his fingers pressed against her skull, felt the tug of her hair through his fingers, felt the swelling of her breasts against his chest.

She breathed his name aloud, and a dim part of her mind wondered if she wasn't asking for something she couldn't even begin to define.

As if her words slapped him awake, he released her hair, released his hold on her and pulled back slowly, as if reluctant. As he'd done on the streets of Carlsbad that hot morning just days earlier, he held his hands out from her arms for a moment, seemingly expecting her to weave.

She was more likely to slide to the floor, she thought. But she stayed where she was, a kinetic toy between his magic hands. Finally, she raised a hand to her seared lips, not because they were in any kind of pain, but because she could have sworn she still felt the pressure of his kiss against them.

"I'll get your cattle back for you," he said as if needing to promise her something.

"Okay," she murmured through her fingertips. She could still taste him. Feel him against her.

"I'll make sure you don't have any more fires."

"Okay," she said and hated herself for trembling, for wanting more.

"I'll even make sure the city and county don't give you any flack about those kids of yours."

And still his hands hovered just beyond her arms. She could feel them magnetically holding her in place. "Okay," she whispered.

"But so help me God, if you look at me like that again, I'm going to carry you off in the desert, and damn everything else."

Jeannie's knees threatened to give way. She didn't—couldn't—say a word.

"Tomorrow," he said, making his words a threat, or perhaps a promise, "it's all business, and we'll talk salary then." He slowly lowered his hands.

"Oh, dear Lord," she said, and dazedly wished she knew how to look at him so he'd drag her into the desert and damn everything else.

"Good night," he growled and stomped off the veranda with every bit as much clamor as Dulce, but with nothing echoing except male frustration and, she suspected, a want as deep as her own.

"Good night," she murmured some four hours later, trying to go to sleep. She raised her fingers to her lips and could still feel him there.

Chapter 5

Jeannie felt the next few days passed in a blur of activity. In between times spent on the road, traveling to various ranches to pick out horses Chance and Pablo deemed suitable for Rancho Milagro, and watching them tug at the strange set of wires and blocks of wood they called a come-along, the days seemed filled with hard work, laughter and rollicky meals.

With each passing day, Jeannie believed the ranch was very aptly named Rancho Milagro—Miracle Ranch. Fences seemed magically mended, the drive effortlessly widened, extra fire walls and flash-flood ditches added along the road leading into the place.

She didn't have to look far to know who was responsible for all the wonderful changes at Milagro—one easygoing rodeo cowboy named Chance Salazar.

Studying them at the dinner table, little José giggling and slapping at Pablo's tickling hand, Dulce leaning forward, her eyes alight with excitement over the prospect of riding a horse the next morning, Chance idly twirling a glass of Merlot, a small smile playing on his lips, Jeannie felt a moment of undiluted contentment. She clasped her hands in her lap, almost as if in prayer, wishing this peace could last forever.

"Which horse do you think I should ride, Chance?" Dulce asked.

"Which one do you want to ride?"

"Oh, man. You're gonna let me choose? Then it's Diablo." The girl all but bounced in her chair.

"You've got a pretty good eye for horses," Chance said, not looking at her.

Jeannie suspected there was nothing offhand in his casual stance, that he did it to make Dulce feel more comfortable with him. It was a gift he had, a rather offhand gallantry that made both animal and human seek his company.

Chance continued, "He's the best of the lot we hauled in here this afternoon. And I probably wouldn't have noticed him in the back of the Jacksons' corral if you hadn't pointed him out." He looked at the girl finally. "Good call." He nodded and smiled at her.

Dulce ducked her face at the compliment, a happy blush showing through the white powder on her cheeks. "I just thought he was pretty."

Chance raised his eyes and met Jeannie's. Her breath snagged in her throat as if he'd caressed her instead of just raising an eyebrow. "And why are you smiling so wistfully over there, *señora?*" he asked softly.

"I'm just so happy Dulce is tickled over riding tomorrow." She wished she hadn't blurted her thoughts when she saw Dulce's face harden and her lower lip jut out in a sulk. What had she said to make the girl unhappy?

She forced her hands apart and reached for her wine. She held up her glass, ignoring her trembling hand. ''Here's to choosing fine horseflesh and riding Diablo tomorrow.''

''Oh, get a grip.'' Dulce slapped her hand on the table and pushed away from the suddenly silent group. ''You probably wish I'd fall off and break my neck, then you wouldn't have to worry about me anymore.''

Before Jeannie could say anything more than, ''What on earth—?'' the girl had stomped from the room. A few seconds later, they heard Dulce's bedroom door slam shut.

So much for prayers, Jeannie thought. She sighed and started to rise, but Chance reached out and laid a hand across one of hers. ''Let her go,'' he said.

''But I—''

''Trust me on this one, Jeannie.''

She looked at him and remembered that split second of time in the Jeep while parked at the courthouse. *Trust me,* he'd said. And she remembered another moment, a flash-fire starlit moment on her veranda in which she'd wanted to trust everything about him and he'd been smart enough to walk away.

''I wish I knew what I'd done,'' she said. She felt wobbly-kneed and very confused. And not just because of Dulce. Chance was too close, too *there*.

''Let her go,'' he repeated, and at the pressure from his hand, she subsided into her chair. ''You didn't do anything. She's just scared. And now she's embarrassed, too.''

''Scared of what? She was excited about riding, so it wasn't that.''

Pablo said something in Spanish, and Chance gently translated for him. ''He says she's scared that she'll like it too much. That she likes everything around here too much."

Jeannie looked at Pablo with gratitude. "Do you really think that's it?"

"*Si, señora. Pobrecita.*"

"He says, 'Yes, ma'am. Poor little thing.' So you just stop worrying and sip your wine. She'll be over it by morning and ready to ride."

Jeannie did as he instructed, though the wine that had tasted so crisp a few moments earlier struck her as flat and sour.

After a couple of seconds, Chance felt it was safe to remove his hand from Jeannie's arm and deliberately leaned back in his chair as if he hadn't a care in the world. However, he didn't take his eyes from Jeannie's pale silence. Only a few minutes ago, her face had held the softest yearning expression, a wistful little smile lighting her glorious eyes.

He thought of the many instances in her scattered notebook when she'd written Dulce's name and followed it with only question marks and seemingly random information about dress sizes and teenage interests.

It seemed the wounded look was fading as Jeannie watched Pablo engage José in a game of shadow animals on the art gallery wall. Within a few minutes, she managed to swallow the hurt, take it deep inside, and a veil of determined saint had been drawn across her lovely features. But it wasn't a veil of acceptance or even knowledge of young Dulce.

Chance wondered if it might benefit the two of them—and everyone else on the place—if he clued Jeannie in on what he'd perceived, that Dulce baited her the most and with the greatest success. It was as if every hurt that reflected on Jeannie's too-readable face became a personal triumph in Dulce's skirmishes with her new guardian. The girl collected Jeannie's frowns of distress like spoils in an unnamed war.

And he wondered if he could possibly let Jeannie know that she and Dulce were two of a kind. Dulce bristled, jousted and wore her emotions beneath a mask of garish makeup and defensive rejection. Jeannie blinked back tears when Dulce jabbed or pricked and hid behind the mask of being Rancho Milagro's caregiver.

They'd each found a safety zone that worked for her, and they clung to their safety desperately. Someone or something had hurt Jeannie every bit as badly as young Dulce had been abused. Abandonment shone clearly from both sets of eyes.

José giggled over a shadow donkey Pablo made buck across the wall. Jeannie smiled, but Chance could see that the hurt lingered.

"So are you going to try out one of the horses tomorrow morning?" he asked.

"Who, me?" Jeannie asked, turning startled eyes in his direction. "I don't think that would be a very good idea."

"Why?"

"Because I don't know how to ride."

"That's kinda the point of riding lessons," Chance said, smiling at her. "Whoever heard of a ranch owner who can't ride a horse?"

She opened her mouth as if she was going to argue with him. She closed it and looked thoughtful. "I think Dulce would rather try it out alone."

"I think Dulce would feel more comfortable to know

she and José aren't the only people on the planet who don't know how to ride.''

"You really do know how make things seem simple, don't you?" Jeannie asked. When he didn't say anything, she murmured, almost to herself, "David could never seem to manage that."

He'd seen a couple of references to a David in her notepad. "David?"

Jeannie looked surprised he'd mentioned the name, as if unaware she'd talked about him, and a sharp pain crossed her face. "David was my husband," she said quietly.

Chance felt as if he'd been punched in the stomach. She'd had a husband? She looked too untouched somehow, as if such an intimate relationship had never passed her way. "Was?"

"David's gone." She looked at the nearly full wineglass at her fingertips and pushed it away as if shoving away a bad memory.

"I see," Chance said, lying. *Gone* sounded like a sad euphemism for *deceased,* but it could also be that her husband had left her. Either way, the expression on her face told him it had cost her everything she held dear. He'd never loved anyone so deeply, so completely that it had left him with lost, despairing eyes. And he found himself hating this missing David, and worse, discovered he didn't like hearing another man's name on her lips.

With real effort, he resisted the urge to take her hand in his. Ever since that night on her porch, he'd managed to keep his sanity firmly locked in place, squelching the need to touch her. He'd deliberately left Pablo near the ranch headquarters while he rode the fences, looking for cut wire. He found a thousand tasks that kept him away from the ranch proper, out of range of her blue eyes. The one fire he'd spotted while out riding he'd taken care of himself, making the time away from the ranch that afternoon stretch into hours. During the busy days, it had been easy to avoid her, telling himself that what he felt for her was just a protective thing—a natural extension of his job.

Until the damnable nightly dinners. It wasn't that he didn't enjoy the evenings—it was that he enjoyed them a little too much. They were too easy, too convivial. It was like stepping into quicksand. The hold didn't hurt, but it wouldn't let a man go.

"And you? Have you been married?" she asked.

He thought he might be able to listen to her Eastern voice for about two hundred years before tiring of it, even as her vulnerable face and smiling eyes made him itchy to run for the nearest mountainside.

He liked listening to her talk. It almost didn't matter what she happened to be saying at the time—though what she said often kept him up late into the night considering her words. But it was her tone that moved him. She always seemed to speak with a slight smile, lending her words an intimate tenor, as if the words were only for him.

"That bad?" she asked.

"What? Oh, sorry. I was a million miles away, wasn't I?" But he was lying. He'd been too close, not too far away. "I was married once, a long time ago," he said. "It didn't take."

"Sounds like an inoculation," she said.

"Oh, it was," he said and grinned even as he grimaced. When she looked at him with questions in her eyes, he sighed. "She wanted the big parades and the big prizes. I just liked the challenge. The purses didn't matter. Which is another way of saying we were broke most of the time.''

She chuckled.

It was impossible to ignore her at the dinners, her pretty face flushed with heat from the kitchen where she tried to learn the cuisine from the housekeeper, Juanita. He smiled over her struggles with Spanish and her fancy table settings. Every single thing about her made an evening at Rancho Milagro nothing but pure heaven—and not touching her torture.

The only miracle about the place, as far as he was willing to allow, was that he was still alive after countless consecutive sleepless nights and a host of cold showers. For when she laughed, when she frowned, when she moved, spoke, considered something one of the kids had said or just chewed on her damned food, he felt riveted to his chair.

The fact that every muscle in his body screamed with the unfamiliar aches of fence stretching and riding horseback for hours at a time and his pulse jumped several notches every time she sashayed by him was testament to her power over him.

He'd told himself that if he could dodge the demand to take her in his arms when she was laughing or smiling—as she seemed to do more and more lately—then he sure as hell could manage to rein it in when her sorrow pulled at his every heartstring. He cleared his throat. "So, are you going to ride in the morning?"

She raised her beautiful eyes to his, and to his immense relief, they were filled with laughter. "You're not giving up, are you?"

"Nope. So, are you?" He grinned at her and realized he'd made a serious error in thinking he was even remotely shielded against her smiles.

''If you'll do something for me.''

Anything, he almost said. ''And what would that be?''

''That would be letting me pay for your pickup to have a tune-up. I've never heard anything so noisy in all my life.''

Chance almost laughed. He'd deliberately bought the beat-up '72 Dodge three-quarter-ton pickup before rolling into Carlsbad with his cover in place. A has-been rodeo rider wouldn't have a shiny new Ford F-350 parked in his garage. He'd have an old beater he could haul his gear around in from rodeo to rodeo, and it would have to be noisy enough to let people know he was in town and cadging drinks and rodeo fee money for the next ride.

''I can pay for it,'' he said roughly.

''So can I.'' She smiled. ''So is it a deal?''

''Riding lessons for a tune-up on the Dodge?''

''One riding lesson.''

''A week's worth of lessons, and I'll agree.''

He loved the way she looked at him, half sizing him up and obviously half wishing she hadn't entered a bartering arena with a cowboy. ''Okay, Chance Salazar, you're on.''

He held out his hand, palm up, waiting to seal the deal, wanting to feel her tough him again, if only in a simple handshake.

She hesitated, then slid her palm against his, flat and warm, just skimming the calluses, lightly pressing. Before she could take back the gesture of faith, he gripped her hand and held it tight, flesh to flesh, imprinting her with his demand for far more than riding lessons, truck repairs or even midnight dreams.

And he realized as she raised dazed eyes to his that

he was in way, way over his head, for he wanted to promise her far more than fetching her cattle, fixing her ranch or riding lessons. He wanted every damned one of those midnight dreams.

He released her hand as if it burned him and almost knocked his chair over in his haste to get out of there.

"You coming, Pablo?" he asked, backing out of the dining room.

"Si, jefe. Hasta mañana, José, señora."

Chance only hoped Jeannie couldn't hear his scudding heartbeat.

The sun wasn't cresting the horizon when Pablo woke him. "Someone's cut the fences down by the gate," he said. "I swear I wasn't a hundred yards away and didn't hear him. If I didn't know better, I'd think we got a ghost riding this range."

"Damn. Next thing we get are some dogs for this place," Chance grumbled. "Bad-guy-eating dogs."

"Doreen told me her mama has a litter of chow-chow-Lab crosses. Eleven of them. *Hijolé.* Eleven. I think they're about ready. Want me to get some?"

Chance thought of the last time he'd visited Doreen and had to clean his boots for nearly an hour after the eleven puppies had used them as teething rings. He almost said no, that he'd just been grousing. Then he thought what little José might do with a puppy in his arms, how his face would light up. And Dulce, too, for that matter. The girl needed something of her own to cuddle. But the picture in his mind was of Jeannie lying back in green grass, a red-yellow Lab puppy making her laugh out loud as it frolicked around her.

"Call her up. Get as many as you can," he growled.

"Doreen will bless the ground you walk on if you take them all. But get at least three, okay?"

"Okay, boss."

"Quit that, will ya? It's too damned early in the morning."

"You're just mad because you're lying to Señora Jeannie and you know it's a sin," Pablo said, handing Chance a cup of coffee.

"Telling a lie isn't a sin," Chance grumbled. "It might be wrong, but it's not a sin."

"It's one of the commandments."

"Bearing false witness *against* someone, yes. *To* someone, no."

"You shoulda been a lawyer, Chance. You're pretty good at those shades of gray."

"The trouble with cousins is that they think they can say any old thing and they'll be fine because we're related."

"That's true, too. Why don't you tell her who you really are?"

"And scare her to death? She's happy now, thinking all the problems are over. Why should I wreck that and let her know her ranch has some idiot out there still setting fires and cutting fences and that her hired hands are too asleep at the switch to stop it? That wasn't a slam at you, pal, it was at me."

"I know. But I think you should tell her because she might want to know. You and me, we can't be here every minute of the day. What happens if something goes wrong when we're not there to stop it?"

Chance made a rude noise. He'd thought of the same thing half a dozen terrible times, and the notion haunted him every bit as much as Pablo's fence-cutting ghost plagued the ranch. "Get outta here and let me shower. I'll meet you outside."

"Okay...boss." Pablo managed to duck the pillow thrown at his head.

When they reached the fence near Rancho Milagro's ornate wrought-iron gate, Chance didn't need Pablo's pointing out the cut ends to know the barbed wire had been snipped clean in the center.

"I'll bet anything it was that Rudy," Pablo said, and gave a swift spit at the dirt to disabuse any notion Chance might have had that Pablo held any respect for *El Patron*'s chief henchman and Pablo's third cousin several marriage times removed.

"But at whose orders—Nando's or *El Patron*'s?"

"It's the same difference," Pablo said. "It's all of *El Patron*'s making. He orders, everyone else runs around doing everything they can to get it done before he can complain about it."

"Was he always like that?" Chance asked. "I don't remember hearing too much about him when I was a kid."

Pablo shrugged. "Your daddy had enough money not to feel *El Patron*'s influence. But I'll tell you, that one, he was born pulling the wings off flies."

Chance grunted, torn between amusement at Pablo's assessment of *El Patron*'s birthing and chagrin that Pablo's immediate family hadn't been able to avoid *El Patron*'s coercion. When one of Pablo's uncles had challenged it, he'd lost everything, including his freedom. And Jorge, young Lucinda's missing husband, had been gone for three weeks and not a single clue had turned up.

"The way these strands were cut, we're going to

have to use this whole roll of new wire. Good thing we brought it with us. Repairing these fences is going to cost Señora Jeannie a lot of money.''

Chance agreed. In cutting the barbed wire down the center, the thugs who did it had made sure that each section would have to be restrung and a come-along winch used to tighten the whole. "I hate riding fence,'' he muttered, setting up the fence stretcher.

"Is she rich, then, your lady?''

"She's not my lady. She's the owner of this ranch. That's all.''

"She seems a lot more than just an owner,'' Pablo said, neutralizing whatever Chance was thinking. "She seems like a real *doña*. A lady. If you don't want to call her yours, that's fine. You're loco, but that's okay, too.''

"You know what, Pablo? You can—''

Pablo cut him off. "I know. I have to go down the fence and set the come-along. We should be in television, you and me. You're the Lone Ranger and I'm Tonto. You're Timmy and I'm Lassie. You're Sherlock, I'm that Watson dude who has to walk the fence asking stupid questions. Again.''

"I don't know whether to throw you a dog biscuit or warn you not to go into town,'' Chance muttered. "Speaking of which, will you follow me into town this morning so I can drop my truck off at Salvio's and stop by the office?''

"You really going to get a tune-up on that old truck of yours?''

Chance grinned. "It's part of a bargain with Jeannie.''

"You're not really going to let her pay for it, are you?''

"Course not. Salvio will tell her one thing, me an-other," he said. "And I want to stop by the phone company and give Pete the go-ahead on the phones out here. I'll sleep a little better knowing we're not relying on cell contact only."

"Okay, boss."

"Damn it, Pablo—"

Pablo snorted as he walked beside the five feet of fence still dragging the ground. "You don't need to go by the office. I talked with Ted last night on my cell phone. He says no one has seen *El Patron* at all for the last week. But someone slashed Ted's tires again the night before last. He's as mad as a sand flea in December."

"Ted's always mad about something," Chance said, pulling with all his might on the post portion of the come-along.

"He said to tell you that Jack's wife Cora's getting nervous. Somebody put some rotten meat on their door-step. She thinks it's a warning and wants Jack to retire early."

Chance swore softly. "Tell him to go ahead. Make Dell the marshal for a while."

"Ted's better."

"Ted's fine, but he's got a temper and right now, we need a cool head at the helm. Dell's our man of the week."

"Ted told me some of *El Patron*'s boys were caught messing around with the trucks out at the potash plant."

"Why would they do that?" Chance grunted.

"*¿Quien sabe?*"

"Right. Who knows? What happened?"

Pablo ducked his head to give a mighty tug on the

winch. "They're all...in jail...now. Potash people were smart enough to call the state cops, not Nando."

Chance grinned. He waved his hand to let Pablo know the fence was tight enough. "We can rule them out of this fence cutting, then. Anything about Lucinda's Jorge?"

"Not a thing. What all you want Salvio to do on your pickup, boss?"

"Guess I'll spare everybody's ears and have him give me the works—short of a full overhaul. And call me boss one more time, Pablo, and I'll wrap you in this thing and use you for the support for the fence."

"Okay, cousin."

Exhausted from pulling wire and from keeping watch on the ranch through at least the first half of the night, Chance followed Pablo to the main hacienda for breakfast, feet dragging. He hid a wince as he spied Dulce waiting for them on the porch.

As often as not in the last couple of days, she'd been outside the hacienda, whether it was six in the morning or six in the evening. Dressed in her derisive chains, black raggedy denim jacket, black jeans, dolled-up combat boots and made up like Halloween, she would lean against one of the viga poles like a vampire ready to pounce.

"Find any stagecoaches in need of rescuing?" she asked. Her tone was snide, at best.

He thought of at least five responses his aching muscles suggested, then said, "Only one, and it had an old man and woman with a million dollars in their suitcases." He tipped his hat at her as he walked past her into the blessedly cool interior of the hacienda. It was scarcely past seven, and already the temperature hovered in the nineties.

"So, did you rob them or what?" she asked, following him.

"No," he said, removing his hat, not turning to look at her. "I saved the day, killed the bad guys and put all their money in the bank in a trust fund for you. The old couple wanted it that way."

"As *if.*"

Pablo said in Spanish, "They kept half, that was our deal. You only get a quarter."

In English, Dulce asked, "So who gets the other quarter?"

Still without looking around, Chance said to Pablo, "She's pretty good at math. Not to mention Spanish. What do we do now?"

"Split our half with her?"

"As *if,*" Chance said.

"As if what?" Jeannie asked, coming out of the kitchen, her face rosy with cooking heat, her hair curling from the humidity, strands of it red-gold against the whitewashed walls.

"As if we're gonna wait all morning for breakfast," Dulce said. "What's with Juanita? She gets lazier every morning."

"She's not required to cook breakfast. I do that," Jeannie said. "And—"

Dulce interrupted her. "Yeah, like don't you know what eggs do to our arteries? At the last place I was shoved into, the kitchen witch told me eggs can kill."

Jeannie's lips tightened, but all she said was, "Only if you're using them as bullets." She set a large platter of scrambled eggs, a rasher of bacon and some plump sausages on the sideboard. "Dulce, would you get the toast and the jellies, please?"

"I knew it wouldn't take you long to treat me like a servant," Dulce snapped, but she went into the kitchen. She came out seconds later and carelessly tossed the plate at the sideboard, making it clatter against the wall. "There. Any more chores you want done? I could sweep out the fireplace."

To Chance's delight, Jeannie gave an abrupt gurgle of laughter. "You might check to see how the pumpkin is faring down in the garden. Last time I looked, it wasn't nearly big enough to be a coach, but given a little more magic, one of these days it might happen."

Dulce gave her a sullen glare, but her lips were pressed together as if she was holding back a smile.

José took Chance by the hand and led him to a different place at the table. Chance hadn't realized he'd sat in the same seat every meal since that first evening and felt slightly awkward being directed to a new location. But there was one big positive about the change—he was as far from Jeannie as the table allowed.

"What's this?" he asked.

The boy didn't answer, but pulled out the chair and bowed with a comic flourish.

Chance looked at Jeannie across the table. He'd always sat near her before. The distance should have made him breathe easier, but it didn't somehow. It seemed so family. Mother and Father at opposite ends of a table, kids and Pablo between them.

"Seems José has a new seating arrangement in mind." Chance decided his mother had less color in the bright red petunias in her window boxes on the old farm's porch than Jeannie sported in her cheeks at that moment. He wondered what caused the blush and for a moment hoped it was because she regretted he wouldn't be seated next to her.

As *if,* as Dulce would have said.

"Go ahead," Jeannie said, and waved a hand at the table.

He'd felt off balance for days, since the moment he met her. But now, with a blush turning her such a flustered rosy color, he found himself wanting to pursue the moment, to watch the cool ranch woman become the dreamy-eyed woman he'd glimpsed now and again. And thought of too often, he added.

"Shall we sit?" she asked, and seemed to melt into her chair.

Dulce sat alone on one side of the table, dead center, leaving at least three empty seats on either side of her.

"She's still mad because we get a quarter of her fortune," Pablo said in Spanish.

Chance had noticed Pablo often intervened after one of Dulce's swift jabs, not correcting the girl, which, in Chance's opinion, would have been disastrous, but uttering some outrageous quip in Spanish before looking at him, waiting for a translation.

This time, Chance didn't offer one. He merely positioned his chair so Dulce's side of the table was semi-censored. To his amusement, little José canted his chair "aback" to Dulce to do the same on the other side of the table.

After they'd gone through the buffet line—the morning's breakfast consisted of scrambled eggs, bacon, plump sausages, stacks of wheat toast and an array of jellies and jams to sweeten things—Dulce rudely demanded the salt be passed down the table.

Jeannie handed it along with the comment that she'd

added herbs to the eggs, so they probably wouldn't need much in the way of salt. Dulce looked at her with that patented derisive glare of hers and used the shaker with exaggerated enthusiasm.

"Extra salt's a good idea in the high heat," Jeannie said placidly. "You don't dehydrate as quickly."

Dulce set the shaker down with a loud snap.

Chance withheld a smile at the girl's thwarted defiance and said, "I know we were going to ride early this morning, but we ran into a little problem down near the main gate, and I'll have to finish fixing that first. Then I have to take my truck into town. So why don't we wait until later this afternoon, after the high heat's down, and ride then."

Dulce shot him a dark look, which he returned blandly. When she looked at her plate, he continued, "I think it would be a good idea to have a saddling lesson on the first day around the horses. It'll teach you how to touch them without scaring them and get you used to the critters."

"At least we know if they start bucking, you'll know what to do," Jeannie said.

He flashed her a grin. "They won't buck, I promise you that."

José giggled.

"What happens if they do?" Dulce asked. "Buck, I mean?"

"You fall off," Chance said before forking a large bite of sausage and eggs into his mouth. He winked at José, who giggled again.

"That's just mean," Dulce said, but she was smiling.

The remainder of their meal passed in a fairly pleasant fashion, if one ignored Dulce's winces as she downed her plate of oversalted eggs.

Jeannie felt she'd never been so high above the ground as she was atop a horse. Twenty-story elevators on the exterior of a D.C. building seemed less frightening than sitting a seeming five miles above the ground on a mild mare with the unlikely name of Jezebel.

"Pet her and tell her she's a good girl," Chance suggested. "And don't let her know you're scared."

"She'll feel it through my shaking hands," Jeannie said, but did as he told her. The horse gave a rippling shudder and whickered.

"Is that a good noise or a bad one?" Jeannie asked, continuing to pat the horse's neck and holding on to the saddle horn for dear life.

Dulce said, "It's a good one. She made the same sound when I gave her a carrot this morning."

Jeannie gave the girl a grateful smile. "Thank God. Do you have another carrot for her now?"

As Dulce shook her head and grinned wickedly, Chance made a sound that was roughly the male human version of Jezebel's whicker. "You're doing fine. I'm going to let go of the reins now. Take them up like I showed you."

"No, please, Chance. I'm not ready. I don't want—"

He cut her off by stepping away from the horse. To her considerable relief, Jezebel didn't leap forward in a mad dash for the Guadalupe Mountains. She moved sideways and tossed her head.

"Squeeze your legs a little harder, and she'll move forward," Chance said.

"She's fine right where she is."

Dulce chuckled. And Jeannie realized the girl was having a wonderful time watching her new guardian suffer abject terror. She had to swallow a smile. Chance had been right—the girl did appreciate knowing she wasn't the only one in the world who couldn't ride.

However, when Dulce had been perched atop Diablo, she'd looked as if she belonged on a horse. Her eyes had danced with excitement, not fear, and she'd flawlessly performed every command Chance had given her. And she'd dispensed with all her chains and most of her piercings. "I didn't want to scare the horse," she explained blithely. Jeannie hadn't wanted to think about what that said about Dulce's feelings about humanity at large.

Chance issued a clicking sound Jeannie had heard him make with Diablo, and Jezebel started walking forward. Jeannie gasped and held on. It wasn't nearly as rough a ride as she'd anticipated, and after a couple of passes around the corral, she almost felt secure enough on the horse's back to pry her death grip from the saddle horn. She risked a glance at her small audience. Dulce was smiling, revealing slightly crooked but beautifully white teeth. José was grinning openly. Pablo and Tomás stood in the shade cast by the barn, eyes hidden by cowboy hats. She didn't want to think what the gentle expression on Chance's rugged face might mean.

"Now why don't you give her another squeeze and urge her into a trot," Chance called. "And let go of the saddle."

"Why don't you go soak your head?" Jeannie muttered. She thought her voice sufficiently sotto that no one would hear, but Dulce let loose a crack of laughter—and Chance chuckled. Stealing herself for the worst, she squeezed her legs, imitated Chance's clicking, and Jezebel jumped forward, nearly unseating her.

Somehow, she hung on, despite being bounced around in the saddle like a tetherball gone haywire. After a couple of bone-jarring turns around the corral, she pulled in the reins and drew Jezebel to a stop. "I want off now," she said. "I have to give my insides some time to realign."

Chance and Dulce were at Jezebel's side in seconds. Chance took the reins, handed them to Dulce and stretched callused palms up for Jeannie. She felt a jolt of sharp reaction. Determined to do it on her own, to stay away from touching him, she swung her leg behind her as he'd demonstrated earlier and, because of her trembling, slid right into his waiting arms.

Her legs were shaking from fear and the unusual exercise, and the rest of her body from the proximity to the cowboy holding her tightly to his chest.

"You did just fine," he said.

"And you ride these things when they're bucking?" she asked, her voice jittery. She was far too conscious of his lips mere inches from hers. And wholly aware of how his hand felt against her sun-warmed back.

"I do," he said. "But I've had a little more practice than you have. I think we'll hold off on the bronc riding until you've had a few more lessons."

She chuckled against him and felt him draw in a sharp breath. And his hand pressed a bit tighter in the small of her back.

"It's José's turn," Dulce said, the sullen note in her voice.

"Right," Jeannie said, stepping from Chance's embrace. "Let someone else get tortured." She risked a smile for Dulce a few minutes later and was glad to see whatever new cloud had descended had passed. Had the girl been upset to see her new guardian in Chance's arms? Did it represent something that would make her feel more insecure than she already was? Would it make Dulce feel any better to know it absolutely terrified her guardian, as well?

Chance tossed little José up and onto the saddle, and it was immediately apparent to one and all that José had ridden many times in his life. He was as comfortable on the back of Jezebel as Jeannie had been terrified. Jezebel recognized the difference, as well, arching her neck like a debutante preening for the best dancer at a ball, prancing on light feet around the corral and walking backward for him when he gave some mysterious signal.

Jeannie declined another turn and left Chance to work with Dulce and José. Standing in the shade of the barn's overhang, she leaned against the broad planks and watched as Chance led the children through a few paces. She smiled when José helped Dulce understand how to get her horse to leap from a stop to a canter, all through gloriously unintelligible pantomime. And she smiled even deeper when Dulce said something that made both José and Chance laugh.

Maybe things were going to be all right, after all.

Chance looked at her then, and the smile on his face held for moment, then slipped. It was as if everything about him stilled. And it seemed that all the air disappeared from the space between them.

Her heart thundered in her chest. Maybe things felt a little too right. Jeannie knew all too well how dangerous that feeling could be. No one could know better than she how the bottom could be yanked out from under a perfect world. One minute all was well, sweet and ideal, and the next, police were knocking at the door, hats in their hands and sad tidings resting heavily on their young faces.

Deliberately, she turned her back on Chance and walked to the hacienda. Every step she took was pure torture, as if she were fighting against a gale-force storm. She could feel his eyes on her, a magic cord that made walking away from him almost impossible.

Inside the cool hacienda, she leaned against the door, as if shutting off his power over her.

When the phone rang, she answered it with relief, as though a spell had been broken. She listened for a few moments, then, without consciously saying anything beyond a murmured thanks, hung up the phone. She stared at her hands on the receiver, surprised to discover she wasn't shaking.

"*Señora?*" Juanita asked from the dining room.

"Yes, Juanita?"

"Something is wrong?"

Jeannie set down the receiver and shoved her hands into her jeans' pockets. "Maybe," she said. "Would you do me a favor, please?"

"*Si, Señora.* Of course."

"Good. Would you please tell Señor Salazar that I need to talk to him in the office right away?"

Juanita hustled from the room and went out by way of the kitchen. A few minutes later, Chance stood in the doorway of her office off the backside of the living room, smelling of late afternoon sunshine and horses, his hair matted from the hat he held in his hands, a frown creasing his tanned brow. The office had always seemed spacious before. Now it seemed made small by his stature.

"What's wrong?" he asked.

In the few minutes since the phone call, she'd had enough time to compose herself, to prepare her words carefully if not tactfully. "The sheriff just called. They found drugs in your pickup."

To her amazement, Chance grinned and leaned against the doorjamb. "That's a new one. Did Nando tell you what kind of drugs he found?"

"What? No, he didn't tell me what kind. Does it matter?"

His eyes lit with a genuine amusement that made her feel all the more foolish for having called him into her office. He'd never been in there before, and yet she felt the stranger in it. Should she have listened to the sheriff's words at all? Given her position, she'd had to.

"Of course it matters," he said easily. "Are we talking about a six-month-old prescription or a kilo of heroin?"

"I don't know what we're talking about," she snapped. "I'm not the one with drugs in my pickup."

"Neither am I, as far as I know," he said, and shrugged. "They cramp my style."

"For heaven's sake. We're not talking about your style here. We're talking about drugs the sheriff found in your pickup. Why would he call and tell me this if it wasn't true?" she asked.

"I don't know," he said. "That may be the question of the day. Did he say he was going to arrest me?"

"No-o. No, he didn't say that."

"What did he say?"

"That he thought I'd like to know that his men had found illegal drugs in your pickup."

"Ah-h. It was a for-your-information-only friendly little call."

Jeannie had sent Juanita after him as soon as she'd

hung up from the call, still stinging with confusion over her reaction to him, stunned by the call from the sheriff. She hadn't thought how strange the call from the sheriff might really be. But drugs? On a ranch with foster children? If there were any truth in it at all, she could lose her hard-won foster-care license. And if it were true, he'd have to leave. And wouldn't that be a shame…but make everything so much easier at the same time?

Not appreciating his nonchalance, she said, "You said you knew him. It might have been a warning."

"Yes. But who exactly is he trying to warn?"

Jeannie couldn't answer that question. She asked another instead. "Why would he try to make me distrust you?"

Chance's eyes never wavered from hers. "Caught that, did you?" He shrugged.

"There has to be some other reason," she snapped.

"Maybe he doesn't like me."

"And why would that be?"

"Because I haven't made it any secret that I think he's doing a lousy job in this county."

"And why is that?"

"Why I haven't made it a secret or why Nando is a lying, thieving dog who would rather eat maggots than help a constituent in trouble?"

Jeannie gave an involuntary chuckle at the remarkable description of Nando Gallegos's character. "That rather answers both possible questions," she said, trying not to smile.

Chance didn't say anything.

"So where does this leave us?" Jeannie asked.

"That's up to you," he said.

"Explain how that is, please."

"If he were going to arrest me, he'd already be here. I'll eat my granddad's old rodeo hat if he had anything remotely resembling a warrant when they searched my pickup—which I doubt they even did, by the way. And, if he surprises me and shows up out here, warrant in hand, made-up evidence in the crypt, you can bet he'll be here for one reason, and one reason only—"

Chance stopped abruptly and looked away for the first time.

"And what's that?" Jeannie asked, wishing he'd tell her what it was he suddenly bit off.

A strange expression, one that seemed a combination of duplicity and guilt, crossed his face before Chance's eyes cut to hers. No smile lingered in those hazel-green depths. He all but snarled his words. "I'll stay here all morning and explain anything about Nando Gallegos that you might want to know. But I'm sure as hell not going to explain why with a woman as drop-dead gorgeous as you are out in the middle of damned nowhere, a man like him would want a man like me out of the way." With that, he pushed off the door frame and left.

His footsteps matched the beating of her heart, hard and furious.

Chapter 6

Pablo had been snoring for at least two hours, but sleep eluded Chance. He told himself it wasn't because of Nanda Gallegos's crude attempt to get him off the ranch—though that bothered him tremendously—or the doubt in Jeannie's eyes when she'd told him about the call that afternoon.

No one knew better than he did how hard she must have worked to create this haven for unwanted kids, and how any hint of drug use on the place would shut her down faster than a coyote could snatch a jackrabbit. That she hadn't fired him on the spot, taking the sheriff's word for finding drugs in that old beater pickup, spoke volumes about her innate sense of fairness—and more, it let him see her intelligence, for she'd questioned him like a pro and even more swiftly taken in the logic of his questions back to her.

And, if he felt that some part of her hadn't wanted to believe the call from Nando because she couldn't believe Chance capable of drug use, then surely that only further addressed her fairness. He'd all but moved mountains for her the last few days, hadn't he? And for what? Some aching muscles, sleep deprivation and that pervasive sense of having wandered into quicksand.

He wished he could believe his current bout of sleeplessness had something to do with yet another of Juanita's exquisite dinners. And tried convincing himself it had nothing to do with the way Jeannie McMunn had leaned into him that afternoon in the corral and parted her lips as if to invite him even closer. It definitely wasn't that. And it wasn't because he'd known she would taste of lemon-flavored iced tea and one of the cookies she'd made that afternoon while he was in town dropping off the pickup that supposedly harbored all sorts of evil drugs.

And he sure wasn't standing here wide-awake around midnight after a long, hard day because he'd felt her throbbing pulse beneath his fingertips or too clearly remembered the way her body had molded to his when she'd slid off her horse into his arms.

Hell, it was all her fault. Every sleepless second of it.

From his experience the last several nights, he knew the only thing to tame the restlessness in him was to take a cold shower or a long walk. Since he'd never stripped down, it was a simple enough matter to pull on his boots and grab his hat before stepping into the slivered-moon night.

At the main hacienda, a light burned in one of the bedroom windows, and Chance stopped to stare at it. He knew it was hers. He couldn't have said how or why. He just knew. He wondered if she was as awake as he, tossing and turning in her bed. He pictured her nightgown rucked up to her thighs and her hair tousled across the pillow. He could almost taste the warm, sleepy tang of her.

He turned from the window with an oath and, for some reason he couldn't have begun to explain, tucked in his shirt. He drew a deep breath and laughed at himself. For all he knew, the lit window could belong to José or even to prickly but rather marshmallow-like Dulce.

But when he turned and looked again, he felt that stab of surety that it was Jeannie's. It was as if he could feel her just beyond the adobe wall. He knew it the same way he knew the sun would rise in the morning and that he was a federal marshal with the wrong sort of protection in mind.

He deliberately turned his back on the lighted window and strode to the nearest place to hide in the darkness, the barn. From there, he could watch without being seen. He yanked his hat from his head and raked his hand through his hair before jamming the hat on again. What kind of crazy cowboy was he, anyway? he wondered. He told himself he was simply doing his job, watching out for her. The fact the job was wholly self-made, that the watching included fantasies of her in her bed thinking of him, couldn't be allowed to cloud the issue.

The point was, she'd been having too many unexplained difficulties on her ranch. He was still sure the source lay at *El Patron*'s door, and it was up to him to protect her and to catch *El Patron*. Nando's bumbling call that afternoon had underscored the need for him to stay alert. To watch. To protect. And if he fantasized, no one had to know about it but him.

He slipped beneath the broad overhang of the barn's roof, half angry at himself for falling into fits about the redheaded Jeannie McMunn and irrationally mad at her for not being right in front of him. She should have been there, not some half-baked dream.

Chance jerked open the heavy side door of the barn with more force than necessary and was reaching for a light switch when he heard a man's muffled oath in Spanish. He immediately dropped to a defensive crouch, one arm stretched before him, one behind— reaching for a gun that wasn't there—as he strafed the darkness in front of him with piercing eyes.

"Who's there?" he growled. He could smell the acrid tang of something burning. He quashed the rage even as his marshal's mind outlined possible options. The barn was on fire. He'd surprised one of *El Patron*'s henchmen. He'd stumbled into many of them.

"*¿Quien es?*" someone asked him.

"Chance Salazar," he answered roughly and repeated the man's question in Spanish. "*¿Quien es ese?*"

"*Tomás, Señor. Soy Tomás.*" The groundskeeper.

Chance slowly stood erect, but didn't relax. He'd learned that the house-and-groundskeepers, Juanita and Tomás Montoya, lived in an apartment at the rear of the main hacienda. Not their light, then. He told himself the man could be in the barn for the same reason as he, mere sleeplessness.

But that didn't explain why the man was in the barn in pitch-black darkness. Nor why it smelled like something was burning. Thinking of the small fires he'd doused the last few days and the larger one that first afternoon, furious he hadn't brought his gun with him,

Chance felt along the doorjamb, found the light switch and flicked it on.

Overhead, fluorescent tubes flickered and hummed before flooding the large barn with harsh light. One of the horses stomped a foot and whinnied softly.

The groundskeeper, eyes wide and on Chance, knelt alone in the center of the barn between the two rows of tidy and empty box stalls. On the floor before him was a small, shallow metal bowl with the charred remains of something Tomás had obviously been burning.

Chance took in the scene as a whole. He saw a barn he was growing accustomed to—a barn like none he'd ever seen before arriving at this ranch. As usual, even with horses in it, no hay littered the broad passage stretching between two rows of stalls. It had concrete floors complete with drains spaced every four feet and was wholly without the usual pockets of debris. And, except for the smallish man bent over a bowl of still-smoldering *something,* he couldn't detect anyone either by sight or sound, though he could hear the horses restlessly moving in their stalls.

Thinking about that first fire in the field leading to Rancho Milagro and the murder in Jeannie's blue eyes when she'd thought he was party to it, and later the fear and relief in little José's eyes when they returned covered in filth, he understood Jeannie's rage. He had to swallow an urge to leap across the barn and yank Tomás to his feet so he could beat the living daylights out of him for so much as lighting a match in a barn. Any barn.

Instead, Chance looked from the bowl and the black curls of carbon in it to Tomás's white face. Again, he fought the instinct to bust the man in more ways than a simple arrest. No matter how much he might want to give in to the need, he couldn't. Aside from mundane considerations like outweighing the man by at least forty pounds, he would blow his cover right then and there.

"What's this?" he growled.

"Nothing," Tomás said in Spanish, scraping the bowl with the side of his hand and crushing the carbon curls into dust. Then he sneered in English, "It's nada for you to think about."

"Oh, I think you're wrong there, hombre. Señora McMunn asked me to keep an eye on everything around this ranch," Chance said coldly. She hadn't said any such thing, but he assumed Tomás didn't know that. "I figure that includes a two-bit junkie burning dope in the barn in the middle of the night. You damned fool! Are you trying to burn the place down? There are horses in here, for God's sake!"

Tomás's eyes narrowed at Chance's tone; but something seemed to give him relief, for his color returned, and he almost smiled. He picked up the shallow bowl and dusted his hand against his worn jeans as he stood.

"You think I won't tell her about this?" Chance asked.

"You won't tell her," the man said, half-belligerently, half-fearfully. Then, when Chance said nothing, he added, as if making his point, "What are *you* doing in here, rodeo *vaquero?*"

Cowboy, Chance thought. *Remember the cover. And yet maintain the upper hand.* "I thought I smelled something burning. Then I saw the flames. And I found you in the barn either doing drugs or practicing some kind of voodoo."

Tomás blanched anew.

Chance's eyes narrowed.

"What are you going to do about it?" The question could have carried defiance, but Tomás sounded genuinely worried.

"Let's see. I could ignore this. I could pound you into the ground for the sheer pleasure of it for lighting anything on fire in the middle of a barn. Or I could tell Señora McMunn just what I saw. Which do you think I should do?"

Tomás's eyes widened, and he took a step forward. "Please, *señor*. Please don't tell her." He held out a blackened hand in supplication. "I need this job. Please."

Chance looked from the hand to Tomás's eyes. The man was afraid, all right, but not necessarily of Chance and his threat. He felt a frisson of concern snake down his back. Tomás didn't know he was dealing with a federal marshal and didn't have anything to fear from Chance other than losing a job he'd had only for a month. But Tomás was close to terrified.

Chance let him think he was considering the options he'd outlined, then said quietly and with deliberate menace, "No more drugs of any kind."

Tomás nodded. And more of that unsettling relief crept across his features.

"And you stay out of the barn at night from here on in," Chance said. He saw Tomás was inclined to argue and added, "It's that or pack your bags tonight."

After a brief struggle with his transparent inner-macho self, Tomás lowered his eyes and the hand he'd held out. Again, he wiped his palm against his thigh, leaving a second black streak across the jeans. "*Si, señor.*"

Chance still felt the tension in his shoulders. He held his hand out. "And I'll take that bowl."

"But—"

Chance didn't have to say anything. He merely raised an eyebrow and kept his hand steady in the air between them. He didn't take his eyes off Tomás even when he felt the lip of the bowl curve beneath his thumb. He took it and lowered it to his thigh, careful not to brush it against him but more careful not to look at it.

"Thank you, *señor*," Tomás said, dropping his eyes to the floor.

"Don't thank me yet," Chance said. "If I ever catch you doing something like this again, I'll kick your butt outta here so fast you'll pass yourself at the border."

Tomás nodded a couple of times and sidled around Chance, heading for the door. Before he could clear it, Chance whipped a hand out and snagged the man's shoulder in a fierce, painful grip. "And, for what it's worth, you might spread the word that if there are more fires of any kind around here, I'll take care of the fire-bug personally. Got that, Tomás?"

"*Si, Señor.*" Tomás pulled free from Chance's grasp and rushed from the barn as if on fire.

Chance listened to the groundskeeper's retreat and stared thoughtfully at the bowl in his hand. He held it up and sniffed at it. It wasn't marijuana, and judging by the lack of powder on Tomás's face, it wasn't garden-variety cocaine or crack, either. No hint of an alcohol base or other telltale signatures of accelerant. But if it wasn't drugs, and it wasn't a fire starter, what the hell was Tomás burning in a shallow kitchen bowl alone in the dark in a barn half full of horses?

No matter how dark his suspicions might be, no so-

phisticated lab existed in this empty barn—or in all of
Carlsbad, for that matter. He would have to wait until
morning to ship the bowl off for analysis. The home
office would be able to tell him exactly what the
charred remnants might be.

He would have to conjure up an excuse to get off
the ranch in order to send it. He shook his head. He
could almost hear Pablo's voice cautioning him about
the tangled webs he was weaving.

He walked the full length of the barn, looking in
each of the stalls, occupied and otherwise, and went
into a loft obviously never designed to hold hay, but
which could probably house several dozen homeless
people. Satisfied the barn was empty but for him, he
crossed to the main doors and cut off the overhead
fluorescent lights. He stood in the dark for several
minutes, listening to his breathing and the rustle of the
horses. He gave a last look behind him before stepping
over the threshold and pulling the heavy barn door
closed.

The air outside was chilly and pregnant with that
special quality of freshness New Mexico's air seemed
to acquire after the stroke of midnight in any season.
A million or more stars dappled the night sky around
the thin slice of moon. He could easily pick out the
Big and Little Dippers and, just rising, a sure sign of
coming autumn, Cassiopeia.

He thought about what Jeannie had said that night
on her veranda—before he'd kissed her, before she'd
returned that kiss—something about being unable to
pick out constellations here because of the number of
stars surrounding them.

Unable to resist, he looked toward the main hacienda. The bedroom he thought of as Jeannie's still had

the light on. He stood watching it, wondering why it drew him, wishing it didn't. Most of all, he found himself wishing she were aware that he'd put out yet another fire for her.

"What are you doing?" she asked.

Chance swore softly, half jumping out of his skin. "What the hell are you doing here?"

"Funny, that was my question," she said. "Albeit without the expletive."

He drew a deep breath to quell the adrenaline rush her unexpected presence had injected in him and even more ruthlessly slew the desire to give in to the urge to reach into the darkness and drag her ghostly form to his. Instead, he managed a half-genuine chuckle. "You scared the bejesus out of me. You must walk like a cat."

"You were busy staring at my window," she said.

"I'm busted."

"You aren't close enough to the window to fit the profile of a Peeping Tom."

"Not nearly, no," he agreed, smiling.

"So you must be yearning from afar."

"Busted again," he said with a ragged laugh.

"There are only two things I don't understand," she mused.

Chance grinned, enjoying the exchange enormously even while he distrusted this new side of her. "What's that?"

"How turning on every light in the barn would help you watch my window…"

The lady once again proved she was no fool. "Ah. And the second thing?"

"What you are doing with one of the kitchen bowls."

If he'd had any doubts about her ability to handle a bunch of kids, he didn't harbor them any longer. The tone of her voice made him feel about ten years old with one of his cousin's broken toys in his thieving hand.

"I'd rather talk about how pretty you look in the starlight," he said.

To his surprise, she chuckled.

"What's funny?" he asked, a crooked smile lifting his lips.

"You. Didn't anyone ever tell you that he who flirts after midnight turns into a frog?"

"Mom must have skipped that one."

"I see that."

"I'm glad you pointed it out."

"You're not going to tell me what you're doing with that bowl or why all the lights in the barn were on, are you?"

"I'm—a Druin," he said.

"If you mean Druid, I'm not buying it because I don't really see you holding a ceremony in the barn. Especially since Druid ceremonies are almost always conducted during a full moon."

"That's what I was trying to conjure up," he offered.

To his relief and delight, she uttered a bark of laughter. "Okay. I get it. You're not going to tell me the truth."

"No," he said. "Not tonight, anyway." And for some reason, perhaps because the stars were so brilliant or because he could feel the heat emanating from her, or maybe just because something about her brought out something in him, his words sounded like a promise.

"I wonder if you ever will," she mused.

I will, he wanted to tell her. Instead he said nothing at all.

"I thought someone was messing with the barn. Like the fire the other day," she said. All the humor had drained from her voice.

"Nope," he said. And wondered if he should tell her about himself now, so she could stop worrying because he had it all in hand. That the man messing with her barn had been Tomás and that she should get rid of the man, but he'd rather she didn't so he could watch the man himself. He opened his mouth to tell her part of that, if not the whole. He felt the words forming on his tongue. He tasted them every bit as surely as he'd tasted her on a moonless night on her veranda.

"Okay," she said.

And his mouth closed. He wasn't ready to tell her yet. He had to know if Tomás was in *El Patron*'s pay. Had to know what was going on around the ranch. Had to save the day for her without her ever being the wiser. And if he told her the truth now, she might not keep him on as ranch hand. Might not appreciate being lied to. Might just ask him to pack up and leave every bit as quickly as he'd threatened Tomás.

No, it was far better to keep his mouth shut and have her keep him around so he could stand a close watch, even if she knew nothing about it.

"So you were just out talking to the horses?" she asked.

"Nope," he said again and gave a short chuckle. "I'm just an insomniac cowboy with an urge to see where I should park my horse when I bring it."

"And I suppose you were seeing if that bowl would slide under the stall doors so the horse could have a midnight snack?"

He glanced at the bowl and back at her. He grinned. "Something like that."

"And staring at my window?"

"You know exactly why I was doing that," he said, and if she didn't hear the rough honesty in his voice on that one, he did. And it scared the hell out of him. Fast horses, faster women—that had been his trademark for years. Even Doreen had used it a few days before. What was he doing standing outside a fancy barn in a puddle of starlight talking to a woman who wore *vulnerable* like a perfume?

But he liked this midnight version of Jeannie, a little feisty and quick with her tongue.

"That's good," she said, and he realized he'd lost the thread of their conversation. "I'm not sure if I could handle your explanation. I have a feeling there's a lot more to you than meets the eye but I'm not willing to look a gift horse in the mouth, so to speak."

"Straight from that horse's mouth, I thank you," he said.

She chuckled again and, for the umpteenth time, he had to quell the urge to take her into his arms. This time so he could sample her laughter. "You'd better get back to the hacienda before you freeze," he said gruffly.

"Yes," she agreed, but didn't move.

He took a step forward, close enough to her that he could drink in her warmth, the fresh-from-her-bed scent of her skin.

She realized she hadn't moved because she wanted him to kiss her again, to fold her into him and press those fire-hot lips to hers, to blot out the worry, stem the concerns and make her forget everything but the feel of him against her. She ached to have him make her heart race with longing and sweet oblivion. When he closed the scant distance between them, when she felt the heat radiating from his body, she couldn't withhold the sigh that escaped her.

"Señora McMunn, you are courting trouble," he said.

"Yes, I know," she murmured and sighed as he slid his free hand along her jawline and into in her hair. Strong fingers curved around the base of her neck and drew her to him.

Instead of kissing her with the scarcely banked passion he'd exhibited that night on her porch, he brushed her parted lips with a feathery-soft touch. Teasing her with his tongue, cupping her jaw with his broad, firm palm, he kept the kiss almost out of reach. And, where the other kiss had driven all thought away, this one tantalized, making her quiver all over.

She leaned into him, following wherever he would take her. Her hands lifted of their own volition to grasp his shirtfront. Her action triggered a blast of fire inside him.

He dropped Tomás's bowl and scarcely heard its metallic thud when it hit the ground. He pulled her roughly to him and kissed her with all the pent-up desire he'd carefully been trying to hold at bay. His fingers tangled in her silken hair, and his lips mauled hers with furious need and longing. And even as he thought he might be too rough, he couldn't bear to stop, to let her go, to relax his hold on her.

When her grip on his shirt tightened, he felt sharp

talons of raw, primal need lacerate rational thought. He
wanted to lower her to the ground beneath them. He
fought the need to haul her into the barn, spill her into
a mound of soft hay in the nearest stall and take her
with possessive savagery, and then, when the animal
in him was sated, to oh, so slowly discover her every
secret desire.

A stray vestige of sanity forced him to draw back,
to end the madness that inflamed them. If he didn't
stop right then, he knew he never could. And from the
low, throaty moan she issued, she wouldn't call the halt
he needed to hear.

Her eyes opened, and she looked as dazed as he felt.
Her lips were parted, swollen and dewy from his kiss,
and her breath came in short, shaky spurts. Beneath the
hand bunched in her hair, he could feel her body trembling and that deliciously wild pulse beating in her
throat.

"Good night, Jeannie McMunn," he said over the
need choking his throat. He released her hair and
slowly extricated his hand from the cool silk.

"Good night, Chance Salazar," she murmured.
Equally slowly, she let go of his shirt and dropped her
hands to her sides. He could see the confusion in her
face, the uncertainty in her eyes.

And he couldn't leave her that way. It would be
better for her, and for him, if he tipped his hat and
walked away. But when a woman gave herself that
honestly, that openly, with just a kiss—though it was
a kiss like none he'd ever encountered before—it was
worse than cruelty to leave her with doubts in her eyes.

"I only stopped because if I didn't, I couldn't have,"
he said raggedly, and with far too much truth.

As fiercely as she had grasped his shirt, she bunched the collar of her robe in a white fist and clutched it against her chest. "It...it's been a long time since..." she whispered.

"Since?"

She shook her head and looked away, but not before he caught the sheen of tears in her eyes. Something wrenched inside him. He raised his hand, perhaps to touch her, maybe to draw her to him again. If she'd been looking at him, he might have done either, or been able to read her like that primer he'd thought her earlier. He might have known what to do, how to ease whatever pain she was suffering. But her averted face gave him no clue to her thoughts or how to divine them. He let his hand drop.

"Jeannie...I—" he started.

She shook her head and raised a ghostly white palm to stop him. "It's nothing," she mumbled. "It's late. Good night."

She didn't run as she left him. She walked away slowly, her back straight, her shoulders squared, a sad but regal queen in starlight. But halfway across the broad drive, she raised a hand to her face, and he knew she was wiping away tears.

"It's not nothing," he said. "It's something. Something important." And for the life of him, he couldn't understand why seeing her hide her tears from him made him feel worse than a veritable flood might have. And he didn't understand why he wanted to run after her, swing her around to face him, hold her against his chest and stroke away her pain.

A few moments later, the light in her bedroom window went out. Chance didn't move.

* * *

Inside the darkened bedroom, Jeannie stood at the window, invisible to the man watching her home. She thought he could have been a statue, he stood so still.

She glanced in the direction of her nightstand and, while she couldn't see it in the dark, knew the picture of her husband rested there. David, safe and loving and gone from her forever.

David would applaud her moving forward, but he would caution her, as well. *"Be careful, Jeannie, love. Just be careful."* She could almost hear the timbre of his voice in the darkened bedroom. A shiver worked over her, and she looked at the man standing outside in the chilly night. How could one be careful when playing with fire?

Chance Salazar was lying to her about something. She sensed that with every fiber of her being. The call from the sheriff had clued her in to a potential vendetta between the two men. And there was more—the bowl in his hand, a scurrying Tomás running from the barn to the main house, not seeing her in his desperate need to get inside. And the way Chance avoided answering any question directly.

But Chance's kisses carried more honesty than she cared to examine. She raised her fingers to her lips and found she could still feel him there.

Be careful, Jeannie, love.

"I don't know what careful means anymore, David," she whispered against her fingertips.

I love you, honey.

Jeannie gave a choked moan.

As she watched through a sheen of tears, Chance leaned over and picked up the bowl he'd dropped when she grabbed his shirt. He turned it over in his hands once and looked at her window. He nodded, almost as though he was aware she watched him.

She murmured his name when he finally turned away and disappeared into the shadows of the bunkhouse.

She didn't see him again for three days.

Chapter 7

The first morning of Chance's absence was a mixed relief.

She'd spent most of the night pacing the floor and questioning her response to him, her desire for him and most of all what she might eventually want from him. The answers invariably tallied two for a confused present, zero for a future.

She filled that first early morning hour preparing breakfast and feeling a flush on her face that had nothing to do with cooking, anticipating his presence like a high-school girl after the first phone call from a boy, a combined excitement and stark terror. She burned the toast, overcooked the eggs, splattered bacon grease on the floor, then nearly slipped in the muck when she turned for the milk.

The very notion of having to meet his direct and oftentimes quizzical gaze had her quaking. The fact that she wanted to meet his eyes boldly and frankly made her feel more bewildered than ever.

At breakfast, when he didn't show and when Pablo handed her a hand-scrawled note from Chance, she'd felt her heart perform a slow fillip, and took the short message with noticeably trembling hands. She read the note through twice, once because she couldn't focus on the words, the second time without understanding. She looked at Pablo.

His expression let her know he wasn't happy about his cousin's departure. The way he waved at the note then pointed to his chest and emphatically at the floor, letting her know that he, at least, was staying there, made her believe he and Chance might have argued about Chance's leaving.

She'd long since perceived that Pablo understood most English, just didn't speak it, though she harbored a few doubts about that, as well. After he'd pointed to his chest and the floor, she asked, "You're staying here, though?"

"Si, señora," he said, and added something in Spanish that had to do with goats, but Jeannie didn't have enough Spanish to know what he was talking about. However, since it made Dulce gasp before chuckling and José duck his head, Jeannie surmised it wasn't anything complimentary.

The nearly illegible scrawl didn't refer to the kiss they'd shared the night before. It merely stated he would be gone for a couple of days to collect her missing cattle and commanded her to have Pablo and Tomás ready the huge pasture behind the barn. She could make no inference of his use of only his first initial as a signature, though it rankled a little.

By the evening of that first day without him, she felt

his loss acutely. Pablo managed to mitigate the loss slightly by showing up at the appointed hour for dinner with a mat and frame for Dulce's cowboy drawing. Before the children went to bed, Pablo showed them how to set the mat, clean the glass and secure the drawing safely in the hand-hewn frame he must have spent several nights creating.

When they'd finished hanging the painting, though it was alone on the long dining room wall, even Dulce seemed impressed with the result. She stared at her work for a long, tense moment, then turned to Pablo. Her hand lightly touched his shoulder, almost as if she were about to hug him.

"You know, like…that was pretty cool of you. Like, thanks."

"De nada, señorita." For nothing, miss.

Long after the children were asleep, Jeannie sat up staring at the drawing, wondering how she could further Dulce's interest in art, if she could manage to lure an artist to come to the ranch as a mentor or tutor, questioning why the lonely cowboy in the duster inevitably reminded her of Chance.

That first night passed, as had every lonely night for the past two years, with a good-night wish and prayer for Angela and David and, as it had for the past several nights, with thoughts of Chance. And those kept her awake through most of the night.

By afternoon the second day, it was all she could do to sit still over the children's lessons or watch them ride. A restless ache like none she'd ever known gripped her hard and rode her every bit as skillfully as José managed the horses.

When José saddled Jezebel for her and pointed at the grassland surrounding the ranch, Jeannie decided he was right. She needed to get away from the place for a while, even if it was on a horse.

"You want me out of here for a while?" she asked him.

He grinned at her and nodded. Then he led Jezebel from the corral and made a cup of his hands to assist her to the saddle. She took the saddle horn and reins in her left hand as Chance had instructed and, stepping lightly onto the little boy's laced hands, threw her leg up and over the horse's broad back. She settled into the saddle more easily than she would have dreamed possible.

"I think you have magic in you, José," she said. She almost felt she could really ride.

He held up his right hand in a classic thumbs-up sign and grinned at her.

She threaded the reins through her left hand and took a deep breath before nudging the horse forward with a slightly firm pressure of her legs. Jezebel lifted her head in a noble arch and walked briskly toward the faraway Guadalupe Mountains.

Her little friend had been right to send her out exploring. She found the experience a combination of peaceful reflection and pure exhilaration that she could ride all by herself.

Not knowing how far she should go or how to measure the distance by time spent on horseback, Jeannie was prepared to turn around when she crested a small rise and saw a large thicket of salt cedar she'd seen once before when she'd first come to the ranch. She couldn't resist the urge to investigate.

She was glad she'd only been walking on the horse, for the salt cedar rimmed a deep chasm that seemed to plummet at least a hundred feet straight down sharp sandstone and rose-colored alabaster walls. Leaning over Jezebel's shoulder, she could see that the chasm hid a deep pool of dark blue water. On the far side, natural striations in the rock formations created broad steps leading to the pool.

She knew the Pecos River snaked through a part of her ranch. By law, she wasn't allowed use of the water. What about this ground water, however? In all the thousands of sheets of paperwork she'd signed when buying the ranch, she didn't remember reading about a pool of water. It didn't appear brackish or contaminated. It looked as inviting as heaven, and as peaceful.

Closing her eyes, she promised herself she'd return to this beautiful, almost mystical place one day soon. Why that made her think of Chance and wish he were there with her, she didn't want to fathom. She turned toward the ranch and the responsibilities that waited there.

By the end of the second day, still feeling some of the peace her secret pool had inspired in her, she found she wasn't annoyed when Tomás failed to appear for his evening assignments. She was more puzzled than irritated that he seemed to have abandoned all his tasks since Chance's departure. The hacienda's scraggly, dandelion-filled lawn needed mowing, the weeds tending. In a freakish windstorm the night after Chance left, a portion of the back hacienda deck roof had been torn down.

No matter how she and the children looked, Jeannie couldn't find the groundskeeper. Juanita, when asked about him, only burst into tears and hid her face in a tea towel in the kitchen. Jeannie and José left swiftly, leaving Dulce to try to find out what was wrong.

Shortly before dinner, Dulce came into Jeannie's office and plopped down in one of the chairs in front of Jeannie's desk. "That woman can cry more tears than Sarah Bernadette."

Jeannie forbade the smile that wanted to surface at the girl's mix-up of Sarah Bernhardt and Saint Bernadette. "Did she tell you what's wrong?"

"She kept apologizing, like she's the evil one of the universe or something. There was a bunch about how much she loves children and loves you and stuff. She doesn't mean to hurt you. You know, all that Catholic guilt stuff. And every time I tried to bring up the subject of Tomás she about went ballistic, wailing and crying all over the place."

"Wow. You're braver than I am," Jeannie said honestly. "I ran at the first sight of the tea towel."

To Jeannie's intense pleasure, Dulce chuckled. "Yeah, you and José practically beat each other up getting outta that kitchen."

Jeannie grinned at her. "You're right there. Did you manage to find out what happened to Tomás?"

"Only that he's coming back soon. And that he's in some kind of trouble with somebody he used to work for or still works for—she started crying a whole lot right about then. Something about his family down in Mexico. I don't know. Personally, I think she's nuts."

"I can't begin to thank you for handling that for me. I couldn't understand a word she was saying."

The girl was studying her chipped black nail polish. "You know, Spanish isn't that tough, really. You're doing pretty good already. I could probably help you if you want."

Jeannie held her breath. She was afraid if she said yes too quickly, she'd put Dulce off with her eagerness.

Finally, she said softly, "I'd like that, Dulce. I really would."

"Cool. We'll start now. You already know how to say goodbye, right? Adios. Only you say it with a *d*, and you should be saying it with a kind of *th* sound. Like this." She demonstrated, making the word sound as much a prayer as the word implied. "And here's another way, like a shorter way, like saying later...*hasta*. It's spelled with an *h* but you don't ever say the *h* in Spanish unless you see a *j*. Got it?"

"*¿Hasta?*"

"*Bueno.* See how I say that...not like you with the *b* on it. It's just like saying no way backward. Wayno."

Jeannie tried it. Dulce smiled at her, nodded and said, "Cool. Now...*hasta.*" And with that she stood up and abruptly left the office.

And Jeannie sat behind her desk, wishing Chance were there so she could meet his eyes and see his awareness of the miracle that had just transpired.

Dinner that night was a flat affair. Jeannie felt Chance's absence with sharp consciousness, and she wasn't the only one affected by the empty chair at the dinner table, the loss of his deep voice and his outrageous tall tales.

Despite their earlier rapport, Dulce appeared at the table with her chains and piercings once again in place and pouted throughout the meal. José, always silent, lost the sparkle that had been in his eyes since Chance's arrival. Pablo, who'd spent most of the evening pacing the grounds like an angry sentry, jumped at every little sound and whirled several times to look out the dining room's French doors.

And poor Juanita, after her flood of tears in the kitchen, who probably hadn't spoken more than five words to anyone, seemed wholly indifferent to the meal she'd prepared, not as if she was worried about her husband's absence but as though she prepared delectable food only for Chance's enjoyment.

Jeannie irritably concluded that if Pablo hadn't stayed on the ranch, she'd have thought she'd imagined Chance's coming there at all, so complete was the reversion to the time before he'd come. Except for the magical spot she'd found that afternoon and that halcyon moment when Dulce talked with her, chuckled and taught her a couple of words in Spanish, all without swearing, anger or sullenness.

After dinner, Jeannie made copious notes in her pad, trying to focus on things to do around the ranch. Instead, she always went straight to random snippets about the man who wasn't there. The way he walked, as if he and the very earth had worked out a partnership years ago so he need never look down. The way he could stand so still that even the wind couldn't ruffle his hair. And the way he made the blood in her veins turn to champagne and her skin to liquid fire.

By the third day, she crossed a border from restless to angry with Chance for pulling such a fast fade. Finding her cattle was an excuse to light out, to disappear when she needed him most, she told herself. That she'd not given him any sign—other than an impassioned and wholly abandoned kiss—that she wanted him to stay on a more permanent basis was wholly irrelevant. That she'd never thanked him for pitching in with the children, helping her with the recalcitrant Tomás or praising Juanita didn't matter in the wake of his abandonment of the ranch and its inhabitants, who needed him.

When her constant vigilance finally paid off and her ears picked up the smooth rattle of Chance's truck, she was the only one of the household who didn't run to greet him.

Dulce called to him, "Hey, Chance! It's about time!"

Pablo yelled something in Spanish.

Juanita ran from the kitchen, pans clattering.

And Jeannie sank to the sofa in the living room and fought tears. As angry with herself as she was at him, she blinked at the vigas on the ceiling. She knew she was being ridiculous. He'd said he'd be gone three days. He came back in precisely that amount of time. It was simple. A complicated man he might be, hiding something from her he almost certainly was, but he did make things simple. And he was back.

Unlike David, who left taking baby Angela out for ice cream at seven o'clock in the morning—"Whoever heard of ice cream at such an hour? And taking the baby?" she'd heard someone asking at the reception following the funeral, not considering the fact that he might have taken a teething child out of the house to let a very tired mother catch a few seconds' respite—and whose consideration had resulted in his never coming home again.

"Jeannie?"

She jerked her head down, not wanting him to know she'd been so worried about him, felt so abandoned by him she'd nearly cried in relief at his return. She didn't turn. She closed her notebook. "Oh, hello. You're back, then?"

"I'm back. I thought you might want to see what I brought with me."

"Whatever it is, I'm sure it's fine," she said.

"What's wrong?" he asked.

A thousand things, she thought, *and every one of them your fault.* "Nothing," she lied. "Why?"

"You're not turning around, for one thing," he said. "And for another, I can't hold on to this much longer."

She couldn't help facing him at that, and stilled when she saw him.

He filled the hacienda living room with his solid silhouette. He stepped forward out of the shadows. She gasped.

He held a squirming fluffy red-brown puppy in his arms, tail beating Chance's broad chest and huge paws scrambling to gain freedom. A pink tongue with one black dot on it lolled from the pup's grinning mouth.

But it was Chance who had torn the gasp from her. He had a cut lip, a black eye, and his nose was at least two sizes larger than it had been before.

"What happened?" she asked, moving forward, hand out involuntarily.

"Doreen's mama's dog had eleven puppies. She sent some home with me." Chance stepped closer to her. Before she could say anything, he deposited the puppy in her arms. "This one's yours."

The puppy wriggled up her chest and excitedly licked at her face and ears. Despite herself, she chuckled.

"It's a boy," Chance said. "Part chow chow, part Lab."

She held the pup tightly against her breasts and raised her chin to avoid its avid tongue. She narrowed her eyes at Chance. "Did Doreen's mama put up that much of a fight?" she asked.

Chance gave a grunt that might have passed as a laugh before his lip was mauled. "Took me out before the second round,'' he said. He winced even as he grinned at her.

"How many puppies did she make you take?"

"Four."

"Four!"

"One each for Dulce and José. That one there is for you."

A strange sensation coursed through her, an odd feeling of thawing, as if some icy barrier deep inside her had been abruptly subjected to intense heat. "And the last one?" she asked through a constricted throat.

"For the other kids you'll have coming here soon."

Damn the man. He was secretive and open, complex and simple. How could a woman maintain defenses against the onslaught such contrasts presented?

"Now come outside," he said.

"There's more?"

"Isn't there always?" he said and lightly touched a swollen hand to the small of her back to guide her out the door. She felt that touch to her very core.

Outside, in the high heat and blistering sun, Dulce and José were jumping up and down by the corral, each holding a squirming puppy. A grinning Pablo was manhandling another wriggling pup as he swung open the wide gate to the back pasture.

And the long, winding road leading into the ranch was filled to capacity with at least two hundred bawling cattle sauntering toward the ranch.

Jeannie felt the blood draining from her face as she stared at the cattle and the two strange cowboys herding them toward the corral. Chance had found the ranch's cattle, and he'd brought them back to her.

As he'd promised.

She shifted her gaze to the battered man standing

beside her on the porch. "You found the cattle," she said unnecessarily.

"I did."

She buried her face in the soft fur of the puppy's neck. He'd come back. And he'd brought her cattle. And he looked as though he'd gone through hell to do both. "How does Doreen's mama look?"

"What? Oh." He gave a ragged chuckle. "Better than I do. But you'll find out soon enough yourself. She's one of the gals on the horses. The other one's Doreen. They've been looking for an excuse to get out here. Flora was one of the rodeo queens back in her day, and Doreen's one of the best on a horse I've ever met."

Once Jeannie looked closer, she could see that the cowboys herding the cattle were indeed women. "You're not going to tell me how you got that face, are you?" she asked softly.

"I reckon it has something to do with genetics," he said blandly.

She choked back a laugh.

"I love it when you do that," he said. "Try to hide a laugh. But I look forward to hearing you just up and laugh right out loud one of these days."

Jeannie felt a shock wave of warmth course through her at his words. And the fact that he wasn't looking at her, was watching the cattle being driven through the corral to the back pasture, made them seem off-hand, unimportant. But she knew he meant what he said. And the quiet tone in which he'd spoken made the words carry greater import.

"Have you seen a doctor?" she asked.

"Nothing a doc could do. Doreen's mama put wool on it."

"Wool?"

"Old Spanish custom. It's supposed to make the swelling go down."

"Doesn't look like it worked very well," Jeannie muttered.

"No? You should have seen it before the yarn."

She hid a chuckle in the puppy's fur. She allowed a few seconds to pass before saying, "I see you have your pickup back."

"Yup. And surprise, surprise, no drugs inside it."

Jeannie didn't answer, but had to wonder how Nando Gallegos's face might be looking that hot August afternoon.

If Jeannie had thought dinners at Rancho Milagro rollicky before, those nights were deadly stodgy compared with the night Chance returned bringing Doreen and her mother, Anna, with him.

Doreen and Anna both talked at once and in decibels loud enough to shake the dishes on the table. They spoke in a jumbled mix of southwestern jargon and twang, English and Spanish that left Jeannie breathless with wonder.

Anna engaged Dulce in a rapid-fire grilling that left the girl grinning and talking more than Jeannie had ever heard. Doreen teased Pablo and made his face flush dark red, and José giggled at whatever she'd said in Spanish.

Chance was somewhat quiet. A smile lingered in his hazel-green eyes, and more often than not, Jeannie would look across the table at him to find his bruised face turned in her direction, studying her, his lips curved in a crooked grin and an expression on his battered face she could only interpret as tender.

The puppies barked and whined from the makeshift pen the children had rigged on the front porch. Anna urged the party to ignore the pups while Dulce kept looking at the door in parental agitation.

Juanita hustled in with platter after platter of tamales, tacos and some kind of fried pastry confection dusted with powdered sugar.

In the midst of all the chaos, the warmth, the noise, Jeannie felt truly at home for the first time in two years, in some ways more at home than she'd ever felt in her life.

When, at a cheery demand from Doreen, Dulce and José disappeared into the kitchen with Juanita after the meal to help wash the dishes and Anna took the men outside to check on the cattle and the puppies and to have a cigar, she said with a wink, Jeannie was left alone with Doreen.

Doreen refused a second cup of coffee but helped herself to a glass of wine from the buffet table. "I don't have to drive home." She giggled and sat down. "The look on your face, Jeannie. I swear, you're lucky you didn't take up crime for a living. I'm not staying here. Pablo is taking Mama and me home a little bit later."

Jeannie felt heat stinging her cheeks. "I wasn't thinking that. You know we would love to have you stay. We have plenty of room."

Doreen scooted her chair, flanking Jeannie's, a bit closer. "That's sweet. Really. I can see why everybody's so happy around this place. That girl of yours, Dulce? She's gonna be a looker one of these days. She's got it bad for Chance, doesn't she? And your little boy, I wish mine would learn some quiet lessons from him.

"Anyway, Geo—he's my second husband—he's got

a job interview in the morning and has to have the kids home tonight so he'll be able to get dressed without a hassle in the morning. As if I don't every day of the week. Chihuahua. That's my new way of swearing. The kids and I have a deal, we have to chip a quarter into the pot every time we swear. So far, they've got ten dollars on me. So I'm using other words now. I've got to be home by the time he drops off the kids or he'll panic. That's what he does best.

"So, what do you think of Chance?"

Jeannie almost choked over her coffee. "He's been like a saint," she said.

"We talking about the same man? Chance Salazar?"

Jeannie smiled and nodded.

"Okay. If you say so. But what I wanna know is, are you in love with him yet?"

"What?"

"Oh, I don't mean to make you feel uncomfortable or anything. I'm not out for him. Every woman falls for him. 'Cept me. And that's only because I'm in love with someone else—Ted Peters over at the federal marshal's office. Have you met him yet? No? Well, when you do, you'll see why I'm crazy about him. *Delicioso*." Doreen kissed her fingertips and sent the kiss into the air.

Jeannie didn't have a clue how to respond to that, so she didn't try. She needn't have worried. Doreen wasn't expecting an answer.

"Chance tell you how he got those black eyes?"

"No," Jeannie said.

"But you asked, right?"

Jeannie felt herself blush.

"'Course you did. I knew you would. You're a

woman, right? He told me you wouldn't say a word about it. Shows him. Well, anyway, he got them fighting Rudy Martinez. Chance told me Rudy came out here one day, right?''

Jeannie felt like a marionette, nodding when Doreen nodded. ''The day of the fire.''

''That's him. Rudy's a distant cousin of my cousin Nando, but on his mama's side. And he's a cousin of *El Patron* on his papa's.'' Doreen's eyes narrowed. ''You don't know anything I'm talking about do you?''

''Rudy's the sheriff's cousin and the cousin of someone named *El Patron?*'' Jeannie asked.

''You know what I think?'' Doreen asked her, leaning even closer, resting her plentiful breasts on one of her folded forearms. ''I think Chance must be in love with you. I've known him since we were kids, and me, I've never known him to go fight someone for some cattle before. A relative, yes. Even a horse, okay. But not for a bunch of cows. And never over a woman. Not Chance. And you know what else? He sure wouldn't be fighting Rudy Martinez for them. Rudy fights dirty. He and a bunch of his guys jumped Chance outside Salvio's garage two days ago.''

''What?'' Jeannie asked, startled.

Doreen groaned. ''I'll tell you something, the way Chance was slinging Rudy's name all over town, he was asking for a meeting with Rudy, if you know what I mean.'' She laughed and reached out a hand to pat Jeannie's. ''And let me tell you something, okay? If you think Chance looks bad, you should see Rudy and his boys. *Hijolé!* I don't think they'll be bothering you anytime again soon. Me, I think *El Patron* might back off, too. What do you think?''

Jeannie thought Doreen had been right earlier—she

had no idea what the woman was talking about. Her heart was still thundering in her chest after Doreen's comment that Chance Salazar might be in love with her. And that Rudy Martinez and his boys had jumped Chance outside a garage. She stalled, echoing Doreen's words. "Do you think so?"

"Oh, sure. Who wants to go mess around with a woman's ranch if she's got a big strong cowboy like Chance to watch out for her? Right? Everybody's talking about it. Annie's even taking bets over at the café."

"Bets?" Jeannie asked faintly. "On what?"

"There's three things, actually. One, is *El Patron* going to retaliate? She's taking two-to-one odds on that one. And two, is Chance Salazar a captured man?" Doreen gave Jeannie another pat on her arm. "And *três,* is Nando right that Rancho Milagro is haunted?"

"Haunted?"

"Me, I bet no on the first and yes on the second two. So I'm counting on you, because I put up five dollars. That's a week's lunch money for the kids—I get a subsidy. So, if you don't mind giving me some help, I surely would thank you for it."

Jeannie didn't know whether to laugh or walk away from the table in utter confusion. "How am I supposed to help?" she asked.

"You give me the inside story. I place another couple of bets at Annie's. The kids have free lunch a whole semester. So what do you say?" Doreen asked. "You gonna nab him? Chance, I mean."

Jeannie gave up and laughed.

Doreen beamed at her. "There, I knew you would be a good sport. Want me to place a bet for you, too?"

Jeannie couldn't help it. She laughed all the harder.

* * *

On the veranda, watching Anna and Pablo walking together in the distance, Chance stood in the open French door to the dining room. His fists were curled as he listened to Doreen's babble. Fighting Rudy and his gang had been easier than standing outside this door listening to Doreen. He wanted to tell Jeannie that Doreen wasn't usually like that, that she'd obviously had a snoot full. And he wanted to gather Doreen up and take her to Ted Peters's house and deposit her on the doorstep. And he wanted to crawl into the nearest hole and stay there for a century or two. Just as he was steeling himself to enter the dining room to interrupt the dreadful diatribe, he heard the unfamiliar sound of Jeannie's laughter ripple through the open door.

Her laughter played on his skin like a fine hand on a guitar, creating a delicate, haunting melody that danced over him. And when she began to laugh harder, a rich, hearty contralto that somehow suited her as perfectly as flowers matched summer, he felt something inside him snap. God, he wanted her. It couldn't be less complicated than that. He just wanted her.

Chapter 8

Pablo assisted a much inebriated and giggling Doreen and her very sober but laughing mother to Chance's pickup.

Although nowhere as intoxicated, a still chuckling Jeannie hugged both women and invited them back as soon as they could possibly make it out that far.

Chance couldn't help but smile when Doreen said Jeannie could bet on it, and all three women started laughing again. And he chuckled as Doreen hung out the window of his pickup waving frantically and shouting a hundred invitations to come to her mama's house, or pleas for Jeannie to allow her to bring her mama out there again or to take her children as boarders.

Jeannie stepped against him, lifting her hand in farewell. She rested her shoulder against his. In a lifetime of having people try to couple him with another—with women pulling every trick in the book from having their mothers drop by his mother's house with coffee cake, to calling him telling him they were thinking of knitting booties—he'd never had anyone merely lean against him unconsciously. And unknowingly make them a couple.

His arm felt heavy as he lifted it to wrap around her, heavy with portent, with meaning, and yet it seemed a reflex. She stayed where she was against his chest, then lowered her head to his collarbone, one of her slender hands sliding behind his back to hook a thumb into his belt, the other still waving in the cool August night air, though her guests couldn't possibly see her anymore.

He drew her closer, cradling her beneath his arm, enfolding her in his embrace. *Now. Tell her now,* he told himself. *Tell her you've been lying to her and are here only for a job, but not the job she thinks you're doing.*

The truck's taillights grew smaller as they disappeared down the road.

"I like Doreen," Jeannie said, and lowered the hand she'd been waving to his chest. "She's crazy, but I really like her."

"I'm glad," he murmured against her hair. And he pressed a kiss against the red curly silk.

She sighed, ran her hand to his chin and caressed him softly, almost playfully. Then he felt her slowly stiffen, as if waking from a dream. As if just then realizing who he was. That he was Chance and not someone else. He'd never felt so slapped in his entire life.

"Jeannie?" he asked, lifting his hand to her cheek.

"I'm sorry," she said, stepping from his embrace. "I'm so sorry."

"I'm not, and you said that. But I don't understand why. What are you sorry about?"

"I just...I can't..." She raised a hand as though it held the answers he sought.

"You can't what?"

"I can't do this," she said, and waved her hand again, as though *this* encompassed the two of them, the ranch and all the stars above. "Please don't ask me to explain. I just can't. I can't even talk about it, okay?"

Chance wanted to tell her it wasn't okay, that she owed him some kind of explanation. That he wanted her so damned badly he actually ached with the longing.

He wanted to shout at her that he'd fought Rudy Martinez for her sake. And he'd brought her damned cattle home. He'd been through hell and back just for her. For her to...what? To want him because of it? What kind of a crazy need was that?

The unfairness of making demands, any demands, given his lies to her, his determination to ride out of there when her troubles were solved, stopped him cold.

"I don't understand," he said. "But I won't press it."

"Thank you," she said. "That's the way we'd better leave it."

"Fine."

"I'm sorry, Chance," she said. But she didn't look sorry, she only looked troubled.

He wanted to reach for her, knowing she'd feel how right they were together, but he couldn't in the face of her withdrawal. Wouldn't in the face of his need for freedom.

But he was still angry. "Good night then, ma'am." He tipped his hat in an abrupt dismissal and brushed past her. Frustration measured his footsteps. A sense of having acted the cad dogged his shadow. A desire to turn around, march back and sweep her into his arms and kiss her senseless made him swear aloud in self-disgust.

What kind of a man was he? A normal healthy man, for sure, with all a normal healthy male's wants and needs. But Jeannie wasn't the kind of woman a man took for a night's pleasure and rode away from with a smile on his lips. She was the kind a man took home, for God's sake, to introduce to his crazy family. She was the kind of woman a man built sunporches for, took day jobs for, settled down for.

And he wasn't that kind of a man. He was a federal marshal, a rogue, an independent rider who went his own way at the end of a job and left the pretty ranch owner in the fading sunlight.

And that was the biggest bunch of baloney he'd ever spouted to himself in his whole vagabond life.

But it didn't change the fact that he wasn't a man with any inclination to settle down and stay in one place with one woman. His mind conjured up that dream image of Jeannie lying back on green grass, her puppy jumping around her.

His steps slowed.

He pictured her arm thrown over her head, her curling hair strewn across the thick grass, her blue eyes unclouded and shining with happiness. She turned her head and smiled at him. A welcoming smile.

The night seemed to shimmer around him. He drew to a halt and stood there, wrestling with himself, fighting both the need to turn around and the urge to disappear into the safety of the bunkhouse.

He heard the front door of the hacienda close and, the decision lifted from him, he turned. The veranda, empty except for the sleeping puppies, was bathed in the soft yellow glow of the dining room lights. Within seconds, even that was gone.

"Ah, Jeannie. I'm sorry, too," he whispered.

Jeannie felt as if she was underwater as she watched José performing a host of tricks astride Doreen's horse, Tequila, while Chance assisted a much-changed Dulce in the saddling of Diablo. Everything happened in slow motion and was weighted down with early morning sunlight and adult tension.

She hadn't slept much the night before, between hearing David's cautionary warnings and replaying the moment Chance's bruised lips tightened and he tipped his hat at her and walked away as if she had slapped him.

How could she possibly explain the desire she felt for him, the guilt she had for wanting him at all and the fear that threatened to overwhelm her every time she let her mind travel as far as kissing him? She couldn't allow herself the luxury of getting too close to another person, no matter how much she might crave it. She'd happily laid her heart bare with David and with her baby, Angela. She'd held nothing back, kept no secret hiding place in her heart or in her soul. And when David had taken Angela out that cold, December morning, he'd unwittingly promised to be right back. It wasn't his fault he hadn't been allowed to live up to that promise. He wasn't to blame for some idiot careening into their car, killing them both. But fault didn't mean anything when his widow's soul had been shattered, her heart torn asunder and her sanity left in jeopardy.

And it wasn't Chance's fault she couldn't give in to the desire to have a man hold her again, to have him touch her, warm her, steal her away from her ever-present loss. She couldn't possibly begin to explain why she didn't dare let herself trust so deeply again, why she wouldn't open herself to the kind of agony such trust could bring.

"How am I supposed to be able to get the girth tight?" Dulce was asking Chance. "I'm not a muscle man like you."

Jeannie felt the girl's tone pull her from her heavy thoughts. It was definitely sultry rather than sullen. She suddenly realized Dulce had dispensed with every piercing, and her makeup was subdued, almost fresh looking. Her clothing, while decidedly different for Dulce, was nothing less than markedly seductive. She wore a short, formfitting tank top that scarcely came below her braless breasts. Her jeans appeared painted on.

Doreen had warned her, and Jeannie had witnessed the subtle signs before that Dulce had a crush on Chance. As Doreen had remarked, who didn't...with the possible exception of Doreen.

Jeannie sighed. She'd have to say something to Dulce. But what? How, without destroying the precious rapport they were beginning to establish? The time certainly wasn't the present, and never in front of Chance. That would be the ultimate disaster.

"Are you riding this morning, *señora?*" Chance asked her, his hat shading his green eyes.

Dulce interjected before Jeannie could answer. "She doesn't like horses the way we do, Chance." She stepped closer to the man and deliberately flicked his chest with freshly painted nails.

Chance seemed unaware of the effect he was having

on the girl—but he seemed equally oblivious to the storm the girl was trying to wreak on him.

Jeannie hadn't realized she'd been holding her breath until she saw him turn from Dulce and check the saddle girth again, then bend and cup his hands to heft the girl onto Diablo's back.

Dulce clutched Chance's shoulder as he tossed her into the saddle. She didn't let go until he handed her the reins and stepped back. "Thank you. You make me feel like I could fly." She purred the words at him.

If it hadn't been so painful to watch a fledgling's attempt at seduction, it might have been humorous, Jeannie thought. Thankfully, Chance remained impervious to the blatant girlish sexuality.

"I think my stirrup is too long," Dulce called as Chance started to walk away. "Can you help me, Chance?" She removed her foot from the stirrup and held her leg straight out, a perfect line of sixteen-year-old symmetry.

Chance grabbed the stiffened limb and pulled it down until it passed the stirrup. He pressed her ankle against the leather and metal. "Looks just right," he said, and guided the toe of Dulce's tennis shoe into the saddle's stirrup. "Now give her some leg pressure and get her moving."

"Okay, Chance. If you'll watch me," Dulce said.

"Fine," Chance said, stepping back. "But sometime today would be good."

Dulce nudged Diablo into a trot, holding her back erect, her elbows firmly at her waist, her chest proudly jutting forward, breasts jostling with every jarring bounce of the horse's gait.

"Oh, please," Jeannie muttered and left the corral for the cool interior of the barn. She knew Dulce would soon be leading Diablo in for a rubdown and currying. How to talk to the girl about the differences between appropriate and inappropriate behavior, especially when so much of Dulce's changed attire and attitude was an improvement?

The riding lesson was over before Jeannie had found a solution to her conundrum. Dulce led Diablo into his stall.

"Did you have a good ride?" she asked the girl.

Dulce shrugged. *"Mas ó menos."*

"More or less? Why is that?"

"What's this? Some kind of a quiz?"

"Not at all," Jeannie said. She rested her hands on the stall's open half door, trying to hide the fact that they were shaking. "I just wondered if you'd enjoyed the ride."

"Yeah, sure. Whatever."

"I like the outfit you have on," Jeannie said.

"So what?"

"You look great in it."

"Yeah? Well, thanks, I guess."

"You're welcome," Jeannie said, feeling as if she were floundering. Some random psychobabble phrase she'd heard once long ago reminded her not to use the word *but* when trying to modify a behavior. "I love you but" was a definite no-no in the therapy game. Telling Dulce she liked her clothes that morning but there were elements of inappropriateness to them not only sounded stilted and old-fashioned, it had the dreaded caveat.

"Was there something else you wanted to talk about?" Dulce asked, as if aware of Jeannie's discomfort.

"Yes, actually. I think you might want to wear a bra next time you ride. I remember when I was your—"

Dulce rounded on her, her face flushed with dark red stains, her eyes wild with anger, her lips quivering with rage. "I think you were old even when you were a kid. I don't think you know what to do with breasts or legs or anything else. No wonder you're an old maid. Like, duh! You're just the perfect saint, aren't you? Have you ever done one little thing wrong in your whole boring life?"

Chance winced, staying out of sight on the other side of the stall, his fist clenching against the door latch. He was proud of Jeannie for trying to tone the girl down and sorry she'd brought it up. Dulce was just a kid with a crush on an older man. It happened, and if she was treated kindly and set free without scars, her crush would blow itself out within days or as soon as some kid her own age came along and got tongue-tied in her presence.

"You just throw yourself at Chance every time he walks near you. Leaning on him, hoping he'll kiss you. I'll tell you, he'd rather kiss a dried-up old tomato. That's you. A dried-up old something. You hold yourself off from everybody, like you're better than the rest of us dirt. You don't even like kids. You just wanted to do the right thing out here so everybody could see what a perfect person you are. But you're scared of us. You're just a scared jackrabbit. If you'd had any kids, they'd have died just because you would have made them feel so stupid all the time, so little and stupid."

Chance wanted to intervene, wanted to stop Dulce, wanted to shut the girl up, but he knew if he stepped around the stall door, he would be adding kerosene to an ignited fire. He hoped like hell Jeannie would fight back and the two could clear the air a little.

He could almost see Jeannie drawing a ragged breath.

"You're wrong," she said in a tight, agonized voice.

"Oh, yeah? Like what am I wrong about, huh? That you're a dried-up saint or that you don't like kids very much? Like I said, good thing you never had any kids—"

"That's enough," Jeannie snapped. "You don't have the foggiest notion what you're talking about. I've put up with your pouts and your tempers and the ridiculous spectacle you made of yourself this morning, but I'll be damned if I'm going to let you get away with this nonsense. You're mad at me because you know I'm right. You can play sexpot all you want, but when you're on the back of a horse and your breasts are bouncing all over the place, you're going to be in some pain, and by the time you're my age, your breasts will be somewhere around your knees. So next time you want to blow up at me, let me finish my sentence so you'll have some clue what the subject is."

Chance had to bite his tongue to keep from letting loose a victory yell.

Dulce rounded on Jeannie. "Yeah? And what about you being scared of us kids?"

"You spend half your time in this house trying to scare people and then you blame them when it works? It worked at the start, all right. You scared me senseless. But those days are over."

"Why, are you sending me away?"

"No, I'm asking you to stay."

"What?"

"That's it. And for you to wear a bra next time you ride."

Chance took his hat off and ran his hand through his hair. Jeannie was good, he thought. Much better than he'd given her credit for, and she'd been one step shy of perfect before.

"Why? Not the bra—that's okay because you're right, it did hurt a little. But why do you want me to stay?"

Go on, Jeannie, Chance urged silently. *Open up to her. Let her see you. Her guard's almost down now— show her you can drop yours.* And he thought of the night before, when he'd been unable to let her in when she told him she couldn't explain why she'd pulled back from him.

"Okay, that's fair." Jeannie sighed heavily, and Chance wondered what she was doing with her lovely hands. Raising them to Dulce? Tucking them in her pockets? "I want you to stay for so many reasons that I can't begin to list them all. And none of them sound logical. I like the way you champion José. And I like the way you handled Juanita's tears. And I like the way you always have a fast quip on your tongue. You're smart as a whip and more beautiful than you can ever imagine."

Chance thought the absolute silence that followed was almost painful to listen to. But if he moved, they'd know he'd been eavesdropping. And a totally selfish part of him wanted to stay, to glean more understanding about the pair on the other side of the heavy stall door.

"And you were wrong, honey, about me not having any children. I did have a daughter. Her name was Angela."

Oh, dear God, Chance thought. *Stop right there.*

Diablo whickered, and Dulce shushed him and asked Jeannie with that note of sharp accusation in her voice, "Did she run away or what?"

"No," Jeannie said softly. And in the pause, Chance could feel a thousand abandonments, a million pains sharper than anything physical.

"What happened to her?"

"She was killed in a car accident, along with my husband, two years ago."

Chance closed his eyes, seeing Jeannie's bleached face the night before, hearing the pain in her voice then. Now so much became clear in this eavesdropped conversation.

Be kind, Dulce, he willed. *Be kinder than I was.*

"I didn't think that I would be able to survive their deaths," Jeannie said, so steadily Chance knew she had to be nearly insane with the harsh control she was imposing on herself. "Until I read about this ranch. And I knew I wanted to populate it with children."

"So we're replacements for the one you lost?" Dulce said.

Chance winced.

"Not at all," Jeannie said, still with that control. "Nothing could ever replace Angela. No one can ever take David's place."

Chance felt as if someone—Jeannie—had run him through with an ice pick. No one could replace David, who couldn't make things simple.

"Then why do you want me to stay?" the girl asked, the raw hope in her voice as painful to hear as Jeannie's steady control.

"Because I want to know that I can give something again, that there's still enough love in me to give it to someone else. To you, to José, to people who need it so very, very much. Maybe as much as I do.''

When Chance heard Jeannie's voice break, he felt as if she'd broken his heart, as well.

"Don't cry, Jeannie," Dulce murmured. "I'm sorry. Please don't cry."

When Chance heard Jeannie's soft sob, he had to look at the ceiling. When he heard them crying together, he managed to sneak away from the barn before he gave his presence away. Before he gave in to the need to round the door and pull Jeannie and maybe even not-so-silly little Dulce into his arms.

The sunshine was too bright outside, and was made surreal by his mental tape of the conversation he'd overheard in the darkened barn.

He scarcely saw Pablo when his cousin strolled up. "What's the news, boss?" he asked. "Rudy in the hospital?"

Chance had to clear his throat before he could answer. "Close enough. Doreen tell you?"

"Doreen's told everybody she's talked to," Pablo said. "Including Señora Jeannie, I think."

Chance frowned. "I don't think Jeannie understood more than half of what Doreen was babbling about last night. But Doreen did mention *El Patron*."

"Then you got to tell her, Chance. She's gonna put it together. And she's gonna be mad or scared. Or both. Better if she knows ahead of time."

"She has enough on her plate right now. She and Dulce are making up in the barn."

"They finally had a fight? Good. Maybe now they'll start being friends."

Chance wished he could agree. He'd had the same simplistic faith only a few minutes earlier. Before he knew about Jeannie's David and Angela, before he'd heard her stark admission of needing to know she still had love in her, still could love, he'd thought a spat would clear the air and set things on a more even course.

Those were the moments before he knew Jeannie had lost her whole family in one fell swoop. Nothing on earth would ever set things right for Jeannie. Least of all one lying federal marshal with itchy feet and an almost pathological aversion to making a commitment to anything beyond his profession.

"You know that Tomás hasn't come back."

Chance nodded. "You're thinking he's the cause of the fires and the fence cutting."

"Makes more sense than a ghost," Pablo said.

"That means *El Patron* has something on him. And maybe Juanita, too. I think we better keep a real close eye on her for the next few days."

"And what do we do about Tomás in the meantime?"

"I took that bowl in for analysis. Turns out it wasn't drugs, but some kind of parchment paper. A kind they don't make anymore."

"A deed?"

"When you want that college degree, you just say the word, cousin, and someone in the department will pick up the tab."

"And when that someone isn't you, cousin, I'll think about it." Pablo fired the words back. He straightened, looking at the barn. "Heads up, boss. Look who's coming."

Chance turned to see Dulce leading Jeannie out of the barn on Diablo. He could tell at a glance that both women had been crying and that the storm, while intense, had passed. But the weather was still uncertain at best.

He pushed his hat back, the better to see them, to wait for them to approach. Jeannie would never know some part of him wanted to stride over to her and apologize for walking away from her the night before, for not turning and going back.

Dulce favored him with a small smile, all flirtation stripped from it. Jeannie nodded at him as if she'd known he was worried, had known he'd listened on the other side of the stall door. She lowered her head as if she'd known his heart was stabbed and his need to protect her had been foiled by mere etiquette and sheer, hard forbearance.

"She's going to ride Diablo around the ring a couple of times to get used to him, then she's going to take him outside the corral for a while," Dulce said with a bit of truculence as though she expected him to contradict her.

"I think that's a great idea," he said softly and gestured for Pablo to climb the fence with him and rest along the top rail while Jeannie tried Diablo's paces in the relative safety of the corral. Though he rested his forearms on his legs and leaned forward, looking every inch the relaxed cowhand, he was as tense as he'd ever been when ready to fly from the chute on a tightly cinched bronco pony.

But Jeannie took the reins like a pro and, sweet-mouthed horse that he was, Diablo followed every direction with ease.

Dulce joined him and Pablo. "She went riding the other day, when you were out getting roughed up—" she shot him an accusatory glance "—and said she found a secret place. I told her she should go back there today. I gave her something to take there.''

"Good idea," Chance said. "Did she say what this secret place is?"

"All she said was that it was magical."

"Hijolé," Pablo said.

"What?" Dulce asked.

"Nothing," Pablo said in Spanish after Chance shot him a quick frown.

"No, it was something," Dulce insisted.

Chance felt a moment of pure, totally undeserved pride. She sounded just like he had the other night when Jeannie had told him nothing was wrong.

"I just got a splinter," Pablo said in Spanish, twisting his hand and staring at his palm. He made an elaborate show of getting it out. "Got it." He held up his pinched fingers and displayed absolutely nothing.

"Right," Dulce said.

"And do you know where this secret place is?" Chance asked.

"Guess it wouldn't be a secret if I did, now, would it?" Dulce asked. "But you know what? I don't think she's all that hot on a horse yet. Might be a good idea if someone followed her. If you know what I mean."

She stepped away from the fence and flagged Jeannie down. The two talked for a moment, Jeannie pointing in the general direction of the Guadalupes and Dulce pointing at the horse's shod hooves.

Chance watched as Jeannie guided Diablo out of the corral gate Pablo had jumped down to open. He lifted his hand in a farewell wave she didn't see as she urged the large black horse into a swift pace just shy of a trot.

Before she was out of the gate, he was in the barn

and saddling Jezebel. And before she was completely out of sight, he was lifting his hand at a grinning Pablo and a thoughtful Dulce.

He told himself he was going after her because she was a new rider and he needed to make certain she'd be unharmed. He knew it was a lie. He was going after her because he wanted to.

Because he wanted her.

It was that simple.

Chapter 9

Jeannie directed Diablo toward the Guadalupes,
searching the rolling, sparse desert for those few salt
cedars that had marked her secret pool. It had been
Dulce's idea that she get away from the ranch for a
while.

"When I was young," Dulce had said, frighteningly
unaware of how terribly young she still was, "I used
to get as far away from whatever house I was living in
as I could. Whenever I was upset about something, you
know? Somehow, I'd always feel better afterward."

Staggered by the emotions they'd shared, stung by
the thought of how easily Dulce had commented on
how many homes she'd lived in, Jeannie had asked her
to come with her, that she had a special place she
wanted to show the girl.

Dulce had smiled, and her beautiful black eyes had
filled with tears. "Not today," she said. "Today I'd
rather walk around the ranch. Like, if I'm going to be

staying here, I guess I'd better learn more about the place.''

Jeannie's heart still wanted to break at the odd sense of commingled hope and despair she heard in the girl's tones and what she felt inside herself, as well. The strange and heartfelt communication with Dulce birthed the hope, even while the admissions she'd made to the girl acknowledged her ever-present loss and despair.

When she'd seen Chance outside the barn, his face a study of concern and unspoken apology, she'd wished they could clear the air between them as swiftly—however painfully—as she and Dulce had done. But it was one thing to admit feelings for a young girl who needed to hear it and a whole different matter to try to unravel what Jeannie felt for the cowboy who knew just how to make her body sing but wouldn't open up with her.

Not knowing how to talk to Chance, let alone how to feel about him, left her even more confused than she was about the children, the ranch and the future.

She hadn't been holding back from Chance—she'd been desperately running from him. Wanting him and, just as achingly, fearing every nuance of that want. She hadn't realized how desperate the fleeing had really been until she'd opened up to Dulce.

When Dulce had railed at her, all her young fears and pains right on the surface and slapped her guardian directly in the face, something had shifted inside Jeannie. She'd felt anger, certainly, and a dark chagrin, but she'd also been flicked raw by some of the half-truths the girl had flung at her. She had been holding herself aloof from them, hiding behind careful attention and inwardly calling it love but refusing to say so to the children. She hadn't said the words yet. Didn't know how to say them.

But there had been some boundary trampled, some line Dulce had drawn between them in the barn, daring her to cross. Instead of coming out swinging at the girl, she'd opened her arms. And Dulce would never know how much that hurt and healed simultaneously.

When Jeannie finally spied the salt cedars rimming the steep edges of the pool far below, she dismounted and carefully approached the steplike striations in the rock. She found a large, loose piece of flagstone, and manhandled it onto Diablo's reins so he could graze on what little yellow grass existed while she explored her chasm.

She readily recognized the deep well as a metaphor for her heart. It was hidden from view and held untold secrets, even from her. And she wouldn't know what it contained until she summoned the courage to follow the path into its depths.

The ledges were broad and covered with sand and silt. No footprints marred the sand, and Jeannie was aware she might be the first person to discover the unusual well. The thought was slightly staggering until she reminded herself that the massive and famous Carlsbad Caverns to the south of her ranch hadn't been discovered until the late eighteen hundreds. They were considered one of the natural wonders of the world.

Step after step, she moved steadily downward until all she could see above her were red walls with tufts of gray-green growth at the top and a circle of pure azure sky directly overhead. At the bottom, the steps widened out, forming a narrow strip of sandy beach beside a pool of deep blue-green, utterly clear water. She could see rocks far beneath the surface. She could hear gurgling, but couldn't see the source of the water. No river flowed into the pool unless from underground.

Kneeling, she reached a hand into the clear water and smiled a little at how pure she fancied it felt. She lifted her fingers to her nose and sniffed them, then delicately tasted the moisture. It was cool and tasted of mountain springs and the recent late summer rains, a sweet ozone flavor permeating it.

How David would have loved this place, she thought, and listened for a moment to hear his voice. She heard nothing but the trickle of the water. She'd so come to expect to his voice whenever she thought of him, she realized she missed it almost as much as she missed him.

But today he wasn't with her. Not here in her magical place. She didn't want to analyze what that meant. Instead, she thought of Chance, wished she could understand what she felt for him, what she thought about him and why, whenever she thought of David, Chance so quickly slipped into her mind instead.

High above her, Diablo whickered, and Jeannie was suddenly, sharply aware of how vulnerable she was in this cavern, with only one exit. As she stared upward, she realized how deep the well really was and how dangerous her descent had been. Had she fallen, would her family ever find her? The rock she'd placed on Diablo's reins wouldn't have held for much longer than one or two strong tugs. And no one knew better than she did how hidden the well was from even a distance of twenty yards.

"Jeannie?" she heard Chance call.

Her heart was pounding, not with fear of physical danger but with a terror greater than almost any she'd known. He'd come looking for her. Come after her. And she didn't have any idea what to say to him.

"Jeannie!" His voice held more than mere worry.

"Down here," she called. "I'm down at the pool."

"Down where?"

She saw his shadow long before she could see him. It played along the sandstone walls, a sinuous cowboy in black. "What the hell— Are you all right?"

"I'm fine," she assured him. "There's water down here."

"Did you fall in?"

"No. There are steps on the other side," she said and pointed, though he couldn't possibly have seen her gesture.

"Stay there, I'm coming down."

She heard him swear a couple of times as he too rapidly made his way down the steps to the base of the chasm. As he had the knack of doing in a car or in her office, he made the unusual cavern seem smaller just by his presence.

He surveyed her unbroken body first, then the water, then, as she had done, looked high above them at the rock chimney that revealed only sky and a few stray salt cedar branches. "I'll be damned," he said.

"The water seems pure," she said.

He looked at her, his hazel-green eyes piercing her. "And you're okay?"

"I'm okay," she said. "I'm fine."

"You scared me," he said, and the expression on his face told her this was nothing but the raw truth.

She wanted to tell him that he scared her, too. Not for the same reason, and not with anything specific, but just because he was Chance and she still felt so broken a person. "I'm sorry," she said, and meant far more than any worry she might have caused him.

"I heard some of the things you were talking about with Dulce. I didn't mean to eavesdrop. I just—"

"It's okay," she said and moved away from him to kneel by the side of the pool. She trailed her fingers through the cool water. "She didn't understand that I wanted her to stay here."

"I know. She does now."

"I hope so."

"She does. She sent me after you," he said.

She looked at him. "She did? Why?"

"She was worried about you."

Jeannie couldn't read his expression. She looked away. After a minute, she said, "In my mind, it was all so simple. Leeza, Corrie and I would buy this ranch. The children would come. It would be all the happy parts of every book and movie I watched as a kid— *Lassie, My Friend Flicka, Ladd,* the Black Stallion series. Old Yeller would never get rabies, The Black would never be stolen, Black Beauty would never be abused, and Lassie would never be abandoned. And the kids would all be happy and laugh and nothing bad would ever happen to them and they would forget all about their dreadful pasts. One long daydream."

"And it's so far from the truth?" he asked gently, warily.

"As Pluto is from the earth," she said. "I wasn't wrong to dream about it. I was just naive to think it could be so simple."

"It is that simple, Jeannie. You've done it. Dulce is smiling. She knows she's wanted here. And more than that, she genuinely wants to stay. And José—I think he'd find a way to be happy any place he might land.

But something brought him here, and I think he means to stay if he has anything to say about it. Or, rather, anything to do with the decision."

Jeannie smiled, and it felt wistful on her lips. "He's a darling, all right. So is Dulce. It's funny, but by finally getting angry with her, I made a breakthrough."

"So the dream is a reality," he said.

Jeannie didn't answer. In that special way of his, he made it sound so simple. So easy, if she could just forget about the complications, one of which was standing just inches from her.

"Jeannie, there's something I think I should tell you."

She waited for him to continue, and when he didn't, she gazed at him with a question in her eyes. He'd taken off his hat and held it against his thigh. She thought of that silly kitchen bowl he'd been holding in exactly the same way the night he'd kissed her outside the barn.

"I'm not what you think I am."

She shook her head. He could have no idea what she thought of him. And she didn't dare tell him she thought he was probably one of the most amazing men she'd ever encountered.

"I'm here under false pretenses."

She raised a hand to stop him. Whatever he was about to say, she didn't want to hear it. "It doesn't matter."

"No, it doesn't. Not really, in the grand scheme of things. But it could." He tossed his hat onto the bottom step and knelt beside her. "You were totally honest with Dulce in the barn. You deserve nothing less from me."

She wanted to close her eyes to shut him out. His

words, his closeness, made too many alarm bells ring inside her, and he revealed too much of his desire for her in his hazel-green gaze. She felt herself trembling. And hoping.

"Jeannie?"

She closed her eyes. He was too close to her. And she wanted too much from him...and too little, for she didn't think she had a whole enough heart to offer him anything that could last beyond the present.

"Jeannie, would you look at me?" he asked.

She shook her head and smiled a little.

"Why not?" She could hear the puzzlement and the answering smile in his voice.

"Because this is a magic spot," she said.

He seemed to mull over her words, then asked finally, in that gentle tone, "It is?"

"Yes. And one of the rules of magic spots is that you don't have to tell all the truth. In magic places, everything is okay as long you're there. Nothing from the outside world can intrude."

She sighed when she felt his fingers lightly brush her hair from her forehead.

"I'm sorry about last night," he said.

"So am I," she answered, and tilted her head to grant his fingers greater access to her bare throat. And when he obligingly trailed his fingertips along her jawline and traced the edges of her collar, her breath hitched, but she still didn't open her eyes.

"You're so exquisite," he murmured.

She sighed as he lifted his fingers from her. And gasped as he returned them to her, wet and cool from the water in her crystal-clear pool. The sensation of cold water being painted onto her skin with roughened warm fingers made her dizzy.

And still she didn't open her eyes.

She felt his fingers at her collar, at the back of her neck, cool and wet, soft and rough simultaneously.

"Lean back," he said, and guided her onto his upraised leg. She allowed him to position her against him, to cradle her between his legs as he sat down, enfolding her with his body. His fingers kept tracing the contours of her face, then finally, deliciously, magically, her body.

"I've dreamed of this," she sighed.

"As have I," he said, rimming her lips with a moistened fingertip. It was a cool, rain-scented kiss.

She moaned softly and lightly flicked his finger with her tongue.

She heard him draw in his breath with a hiss. "God, Jeannie, I've wanted you since the first second I saw you waiting in Doreen's post office," he murmured, and his legs seemed to involuntarily draw her tighter to him.

She flexed against him, arched to meet his exploring fingers and instead met his hot, questing mouth. He tasted of coffee and carefully banked passion. His firm lips grazed hers like liquid velvet, and his tantalizing hand cupped her face so tenderly it brought tears to her eyes. And he kissed the tears away.

Her hands seemed to lift of their own volition and flatten against the hard planes of his chiseled face. Like a blind woman, she felt the contours of his cheeks, the rigid jawline, the pulse beating furiously at his temples. From his thundering heartbeat to his ragged breathing to his liquid-soft touch and kiss, she reveled in the knowledge that here in this magic place he was as besotted as she and every bit as vulnerable.

And still she didn't open her eyes.

One of his hands held her by the shoulder while the other slowly, tantalizingly explored her every curve, slowing for the mounds of her breasts, stopping at her waist, then speeding along the curve of her hips to her thighs. And, at a snail's pace, coming up, lightly teasing the insides of her legs, brushing across her apex, teasing over her breasts. An almost choked sound came from his throat, and his hand stopped to research with greater intent.

"Jeannie?" he murmured.

"Mmm?"

He deftly unfastened the buttons of her blouse and spread the material wide. She leaned against his arm, allowing him full access.

"Jeannie?"

His enchanting fingers teased along the lacy edges of her bra and dipped beneath to flick an already hardened nipple.

"Look at me." When she didn't obey his soft command, he kissed her again, continuing his quest with a single dampened finger. His hands were chilled from the cool water. His lips were hot with a burning intensity that threatened to drive her insane.

When he lifted his lips from hers and dropped them to her collarbone, she moaned and arched to meet him.

"You have to look at me now, Jeannie. This isn't a dream. It isn't a fantasy. I want to know you're with me all the way here."

She opened her eyes and found the reality far sweeter than any dream. His hazel-green eyes glittered in the strange light of her magical pool and seemed to hold all the secrets of the universe within their colored depths. And lurking behind the passion was such a wealth of kindness, understanding, sympathy and sheer longing that she felt stripped naked and wholly empowered by the multiplicity of wants.

"I'm with you all the way here," she said, modifying his words even as she tried pinning them down to one specific place, one time out of a whole universe of realities.

He lifted her, swiftly and effortlessly pulling her from between his legs and rolling them over, so that her head lay resting upon his forearm and her body was stretched beneath him.

"No doubts?" he asked.

"Not here," she answered truthfully.

He chuckled over her caveat. "Here or anywhere else doesn't matter," he said. "I'm going to make love to you, Jeannie McMunn."

"I know that, Chance Salazar," she said.

"You will," he said, and the tone of his voice made his words a vow, a solemn promise.

"That sounds like a threat," she said, and almost laughed at herself for flirting in the middle of such a seemingly solemn moment.

"Oh, no, Jeannie. It's an absolute given. I want you to know every touch I make with every fiber of your body. And, damn it all, I don't want to just be a fantasy."

"Are we talking about you...or me?" she asked.

He hesitated. "I've dreamed about you far too long. You're driving me crazy with fantasy. I want the real thing."

"I don't know what that is anymore," she said, too truthfully, hating the outside world trying to sneak into this magical, halcyon place.

"You," he said. "You're the magic. Not this spring, not this sinkhole you're calling a magical place. It's just you. You carry it with you all the time. I don't know how. I don't even care why. Some things just are.''

Again, he made things simple. Jeannie thought of the puppies he'd brought to the ranch. She thought of the horses, the laughter, the loyalty he gathered around him, and she thought of David and hard-won intimacy and lost promises. And lost love.

''You're trying to bring the outside world into this place,'' she said, her hands framing his beautiful face. ''Remember, this is magical. I don't want to remember anything here. Just feel. I just want to feel.''

''But it's not magic,'' he said. ''It's just a sinkhole. Just a place. The magic is all in your head.''

''And in your heart,'' she murmured.

''And in your heart,'' he agreed, laying a warm hand in the hollow between her breasts. ''Oh, yeah, in your heart. Take a chance, Jeannie,'' he said.

''That's your name,'' she said dreamily, and let her hands drop to the sand, offering herself to him without words.

''And?''

''And…yes. I'll take the chance. I'll take you, Chance.''

Chance felt as if the universe shifted out of focus for a long, aching moment. Kidding him, she nevertheless managed to give him every raw strip of her heart. He knew he should stop the inevitable conclusion of this strange game they were playing in Jeannie's miraculous, magical well—and probably Pablo's mystical lost spring, as well. He knew she was too vulnerable and he was too raw from having witnessed her tears and having just learned about her tragedy. But with her trusting body lying beneath him, with her humor and her honesty before him, he couldn't.

Hell, he wouldn't. He'd been a fool to let go of her that first evening. And a double-damned idiot to let her walk away from him the night he'd kissed her outside the barn. He didn't even want to think of how lacerated he'd felt the night before—or how he'd ripped at her with his tipped hat and brush-off and his sure certainty that she needed him as badly as he craved her.

Even after he'd left her, his damnable pride carrying him away from her, he could smell her on his hands, feel her pressed against his body. He'd spent the night aching for her until every muscle in his body seemed stretched and pained beyond all recognition, and the longing in him left him tired, as if he'd been trying to reach out for her the entire night and more than half the day afterward.

With her, as with no one else, Chance felt he was always reaching and never grasping what he so wanted. And yet, here she was, if not wholly relaxed, at least lying with her shirt spread wide, revealing glorious breasts that raised and lowered in time to her slightly rapid breathing. Her open arms splayed on her magical sinkhole beach, fingers curled, an odd little smile dancing on her parted lips, her eyes half closed, an invitation etched in denim blue. He knew he'd never wanted anyone the way he wanted her. And he'd never been so scared in his entire life.

At various moments, he felt he had slipped into quicksand every time he was near her. Now he hovered on the edge of a cliff, as if part of him were still on the lip of the chasm. Everything in the universe could change with touching her.

"Kiss me, please," she murmured.

And with no further thought, he stepped off the cliff's edge of rational thought.

With a groan, he lowered his lips to hers, breaking his plummet into the unknown with her taste, her mouth cushioning the free fall.

One hand cushioned her head, tangling in her silky hair, and he used the other to roam her curves, sliding behind her back to draw her up to meet him. She writhed beneath him, enflaming him with her unfettered want.

He slipped her bra straps from her shoulders and with a swift tug freed her magnificent breasts. At her sigh, he took a nipple into his mouth and laved it with his tongue until it was rock hard and peaked, and suckled it until she moaned and arched higher. He rose from her breast only to capture the other nipple with his lips, playing it gently with his teeth and tongue until, as her fingers gripped his hair, he stopped teasing her and took her fully into his mouth, abandoning the light touch.

He strafed her body with his hand, molding her to him, exhorting her to know how thoroughly she aroused him, needing to feel her legs wrap around his, to feel her want against him. And as she readily complied, a soft growl deep in her throat, he swiftly unfastened the button and zipper of her jeans. Her moan matched his as he slid his fingers beneath her lacy panties and brushed against the crisp curls that hid her core from him.

Suckling a breast, tormenting her with his fingers, he heard her ragged breathing and knew he was nowhere close to allowing her pleasure to so quickly peak. He pulled away from her. Moving her lax body as if she were a beautiful rag doll, he slowly stripped away her blouse, raised her then settled her on it. He traced the tiny smile on her lips with his tongue as he slipped her bra around, unfastened it and tugged it free of her body. And he removed his shirt and, lifting her up, rested her hips on it. And he tantalizingly, oh, so slowly, pulled down her jeans, kissing each new patch of skin that was revealed.

"Chance..." She moaned when he reached her feet and removed her tennis shoes and socks before stripping the jeans away. He tossed the jeans aside and drew a harsh, ragged breath when he turned to look at her exposed body. Wearing a pair of lacy black panties that suggested more than hid her from him, Jeannie lay still, her eyes hooded with desire, her lips parted and moist. Her nipples, hard and pointed, seemed to call to him, but then so did every other part of her body. The insides of her elbows, the hollows of her neck, the swell of her hips, her eyes, her lush mouth.

"You, too," she whispered. "I want to see you, too.

He loved the way she watched him as he unfastened his belt and jeans. And grinned a little self-consciously as he yanked off his boots and socks. The sand felt cool and soft beneath his bare feet. But it was the sight of her that made him hard. And he hardened more when she sighed at the sound of his lowering zipper. When he sprang free as he stood in a fluid motion and shoved the jeans away, her light moan echoed his own.

Instead of lying down in her opened arms, he knelt over her middle and began peeling those lacy panties down her long legs. Again he trailed the slip of clothing with his tongue and lips, kissing the places he'd dreamed about, the spots that made her moan and the secrets that had kept him awake so many nights. And after he slipped the panties free of her arched feet, he dropped them onto her jeans. Parting her legs, he knelt between them, running his hands up the insides of her thighs, kneading her trembling limbs, reveling in every silken, freckled nuance of her. He lifted her feet and massaged them lightly, then rested them behind his head and bent to kiss her opened thighs, the soft, delicate skin leading to her core.

He glanced at her. Her eyes were staring, glazed and a little wild.

"You remind me of a roan Appaloosa I wanted to own so badly once upon a time that I spent hours every night trying to figure out a way I could have her. You do that to me."

"A man and his horse," she said, and smiled.

"You haunt me every bit as much as that horse did."

She chuckled. "Nice to know I'm about equal with a cowboy's horse."

"Lady, you don't know the half of it."

She chuckled again, then gasped as he dipped fingers into her honeyed core. Driving himself nearly as insane as he hoped he was her, he lowered his mouth to slowly taste her, hungry to learn all her secrets. With a patience born of nothing but sheer, raw desire to please her in every possible way, he carefully laved, taking in her scent, her essence, needing to hear her call his name, aching to feel her body convulse around his fingers.

As if reading his mind, she did cry out and arch against him. And faster he kissed her, pressing his fingers into her, slipping his free hand beneath her to raise her even higher.

She called his name again, a desperate plea, and it was all he could do not to give in to her demands, stop what he was doing and plunge into her, taking her with all his might. But he stayed where he was, his lips and tongue moving faster, his fingers a counterpoint melody.

"Chance, oh, please, please..."

She didn't know if she was pleading for him to stop or to continue. Her legs were shaking, her thighs pressing against the hard planes of his face. Her fingers dug into the sand. Her body trembled, and her breasts heaved. And still he wouldn't stop, and she felt herself spiraling into a universe she'd never seen before. Colors, sharp blues, reds and glittering white danced in her eyes. And suddenly, and without any more warning that his name tangled in her throat, she bucked against him and convulsed around him, every single part of her drawing inward with sharp spasms of ecstasy.

More in tune with her body than she could ever have imagined, he held her there in that magical universe, drawing every shuddering element of her release into him and soothing her down again.

She murmured his name like a litany, a bridge back to this world, and felt tears gather in her eyes, tears not of sorrow but of exquisite release. And when he raised his head, his eyes were glassy and nearly emerald-green with harsh want. She slid her legs down his back and opened her arms to him, beckoning him to come to her.

He slapped his hand against the water, splashing them both a little, and dragged his wet hand across his face before rising above her, as if no longer seeking permission but demanding access. She raised her hands to his damp face and pulled him down for a kiss.

Tasting the cool water and herself, she sighed into his mouth. "Please, now, Chance. Now."

And he drove into her with a single fluid motion, filling her, calling her name out as he lowered himself deeper into her. He closed his eyes as if in pain, then slowly pulled back until he was nearly outside her again. She tightened her legs and locked her ankles behind his buttocks to pull him inside, deeper and harder. He ground out her name, pressing her breasts flat beneath his chest, thrusting into her with all the pent-up passion he'd been so carefully holding at bay.

He rocked into her, pressing her against their shirts in the sand, slowly and with deliberate strokes that gentled her even as they reawakened desire. His body was as beautiful as his actions and as powerful as the emotions he inspired in her. She ran her hands along his muscled shoulders, massaging him, exhorting him, drawing him to her, then simply holding on as he began to drive into her in ever increasing thrusts. Faster and harder he met her, murmuring inchoate words or imprecations against her lips or the base of her throat. With each thrust, he paused, as if savoring every single stroke and touch. He stopped abruptly, his breath coming in harsh, jagged intakes. He raised up slightly, his green eyes locked with hers.

"It's safe with me, Jeannie," he said raggedly.

"Nothing's safe," she murmured even as her legs pulled at him, propelling him into that rocking motion.

He uttered a harsh groan, one so filled with longing and need that it seemed to vibrate through her. And with his eyes gazing directly into hers, as if they were linked at some level far greater than just physical or even primal, he resumed his deep, slow thrusting. Like an inferno gathering flame, he began to pump with greater and greater intensity against her.

She felt the beginning of another release, the spiraling, coiling sensation that coincided with his flinging her into that other universe. And faster and harder he thundered into her. Calling her name. Demanding she travel with him. And she stayed with him stroke for stroke. Until he froze suddenly, his face pulled tight with agony, her name a prayer on his lips. And she felt him shudder over her, within her. Releasing, pumping, quivering inside her, sending her over the edge into that world of magical colors and glittering white light.

It seemed hours later that the world devolved into this plane again, and Jeannie understood the whirling colors of red, blue and white had been the chimney high above them, not magically spinning but gloriously expanding as she'd arched to meet Chance. She ran her hands along his shoulders and slowly slid her legs down his, keeping her ankles locked to hold him inside her as long as she could.

He nuzzled her neck and drew his fingers through her hair as if combing it, stroking her differently now that the height of passion had peaked and been conquered. Caressing her instead of exhorting, gentling her instead of urging her to climax.

She pressed her hands against his arms to have him sink fully down on her, to feel his weight with no barrier.

"I'll smash you," he said.

"Good," she answered. And it was good. She'd never thought of it before, how much the sheer physical weight pressing down was such a vital aspect in making love, in knowing one's partner, letting him know her. For a brief, almost tender second, she thought of David, of how they were together. But this time the thought came without comparisons and without pain. They had been good together.

And she and Chance were good together. "Amazingly good," she murmured aloud.

"And to think, I spent all those nights when I was a kid wanting an Appaloosa when you were out there somewhere in the world."

She chuckled, and he groaned as her muscles involuntarily clenched around him.

Amazing her, she felt him stir within her, a hesitant, almost playful flicker of life. She deliberately gave a squeeze, and delighting her, he matched the pulse with a jolt of his own.

He chuckled against her, and she felt a ripple throughout her body. And she laughed with him. Around him.

Chance raised up onto one elbow and gazed at the smiling beauty so securely pinned beneath him. "Hold on to me," he said.

"What?"

"Trust me."

He wrapped his arm behind her, lifting her up to meet his lips, then gave a mighty shove with the hand still planted in the sand and rolled them over into the cool water of her magic pond.

She gave a brief shriek and instead of fighting to get away from him clung to him, holding him even tighter against her as he found a footing.

Still locked within her, loving the way she instinctively wrapped her legs around his waist and her arms around his neck, he shifted her so that he could suckle her breasts again. "You're so incredibly beautiful," he murmured around a pebble-hard nipple. "A man could never get enough of you."

She didn't answer except for a small moan of pleasure. She loosened her grip around his neck to lean into the water, her hair fanning out from her like a siren trapped by her own music.

He molded her breasts, nuzzled them, and as she began to rock against him, he lightly nipped at them. And keeping hold of her with his mouth, he lowered his hands to her bottom and cupped the rounded flesh, pulling her more tightly to him, over him, playing with her, touching her, kneading her flesh while he drove into her yet again.

And when she cried out, his name torn from her lips, her magical waters splashed over them and around them. And for a single shining moment, just as he called her name in return, Chance Salazar knew he was in the exact right place in the universe. It was a place he'd never been before and was all too afraid he might never find again.

Chapter 10

Although Chance's watch showed the afternoon had advanced, Jeannie knew the sun wouldn't set for another five or six summertime hours. This was the longest stretch of hours she'd left the children with Juanita at the ranch except for those rare occasions she went into Carlsbad.

Still, her reluctance to leave the magic pond showed in how slowly she dressed, stopping too often to shake her clothes free of sand, to rinse her hands yet again in the cool, clear water. There was so much she wanted to be able to say to Chance but didn't know how. She wanted to give him nothing but the truth, nothing but the sheer, raw honesty they'd shared in this halcyon place this afternoon. But even as she buttoned her blouse and zipped her jeans, she could feel the distance growing between them. For a few blissful hours, he'd almost made her feel whole again, made such a concept as sharing seem possible. But then what? She knew how fragile life was and knew she didn't have it in her to offer that kind of loving trust and intimacy again. And she certainly didn't know how to accept it.

And yet, a very real part of her wanted to ask him to stay with her. Stay long enough to let her heal, let her breathe again. Let her learn how to love him—to love again, period. He'd never know how much she wanted to ask it of him.

She'd asked him to make her forget, to take her away from the world for a while. Instead, though he'd driven her senseless, he'd brought her back to the world. With all its hurts, its despairs and with every bit of all its joys. And, most frightening of all, all the world's hopes. She didn't want hopes—except for the children—and she trembled at feeling them.

It had been difficult to know what to say to him. Part of her wanted to thank him. Thank him for making her feel a woman again, for making her believe in her beauty, for making her feel every touch, stroke and kiss and give those to him in return. And a darker, more selfish side of her wanted to rail at him for making her feel anything. It made her too aware of all she'd been missing, all she might discover if she allowed herself to remain as open as she'd been in the chasm he called a sinkhole.

But it had been magic that bound them that afternoon. The water, the red rocks, the blue, blue sky, the privacy. And Chance. Incredible, magical Chance. But magic always had a finish, a conclusion, and it was over with a wave of a wand and a puff of smoke and the final applause.

What was beautiful and delicious there in that magic spot couldn't be sustained in the real world, could it?

They were out of the chasm, in the harshly lit real

world, and not all the magic in the world could follow them home. If her body carried the reminders of their time spent together, even that would fade with time. And if her heart might carry marks forever, her heart was well populated with magical moments and loves she'd had to bury and lock away in that heavy dark place.

She glanced at the nearly invisible cliff edge, as if memorizing it for a time when she would need a lovely memory, then looked at the Guadalupe Mountains so starkly purple, silhouetted in the late afternoon sunlight. With a resolute sigh, she turned Diablo in the direction of the ranch.

"There's a shorter way," Chance said and pointed across the flatlands to the south of the well.

"That will take us back to the ranch?" Jeannie asked, surprised. She'd only been out here twice, but both times she'd come from the back pasture side, today with the lowing of some two hundred head of cattle to egg her on, the other time without that unique encouragement. She'd come by way of the rolling hills north and west of the ranch headquarters.

Chance was pointing in a direction she would have thought would take them straight into Carlsbad and away from the ranch. She had to look at him, had to ask him how he knew the way when she'd had only mountains in the background and a few hills that all looked the same to guide her.

It was almost a relief to discover he wasn't looking at her. His eyes were far in the distance, seeing things in the desert she might never see. He lifted in his stirrups as if eight more inches might grant him a view of the world he couldn't have seen just sitting there. The muscles on his legs corded with effort of standing in stirrups, and his back was rigid. He sank down and flashed a grin in her general direction. "It'll drop us on the side of the road where we fought that first fire."

Jeannie shrugged and nudged Diablo to follow Jezebel across the flats. "Did you say *first* fire?" she asked after they left the salt cedars rimming her chasm behind.

"You weren't supposed to catch that," he said. "Forget I said it."

"Stop," Jeannie said, and when he did, she turned her eyes directly to his. She realized she'd been avoiding his eyes ever since the moment they'd decided the bliss was finished, the day was drawing to a close, that they had to leave the magic pond. And, worse, seeing the guarded look in his eyes, she suddenly understood there had been no moment when the deciding happened.

They'd laughed together, loved together, dipped in the cool water and played together, but there wasn't a moment when either of them had turned to the other and said, "The magic's over, sweetheart, we have to leave now."

There had been no words. No sighs. No negatives of any kind.

And there had been no promises or dreams of the future talked about in the aftermath of such splendor because she wasn't capable of promising anything other than a modicum of safety to the children. She couldn't offer more to Chance, to anyone, because her heart was too damaged, her soul too broken.

She'd shied away from speaking any of these truths, or even any of the lies she'd hidden behind for so long, when he'd assisted her onto Diablo. But she wondered about them now. Had she been hiding? Was that a strange direction her grief had taken her? Not that she couldn't love again, but that she wouldn't? Was her fear of the future—of not having enough love to offer—a mask for a deeper truth, that she was a woman afraid of loving again because to be open to love was to also be vulnerable to pain? It couldn't be that easy, and yet the notion held a ring of truth.

"There were other fires?" she asked.

"A few. Small ones. No big deal."

"What were you going to tell me down by the pond?" she asked.

He pushed his hat back and studied her. "It wasn't okay to tell you then, but it is now?"

She nodded.

He chuckled and shook his head. "But this is a magical spot, too," he said.

Jeannie fought the smile his grin was provoking. "And how do you figure that?"

"It's Miracle Ranch. That's enough, isn't it? Come on, Señora McMunn, it's time to head for home."

She wished she dared ask him what he was thinking as they rode along, but she was afraid he might tell her in that devastating way he had of cutting straight to the heart of things. And if he told her how he felt about her, what would she say? Either way, good or bad, it would be admitting feelings she didn't want to acknowledge and didn't remember how to accept.

There had seemed nothing she couldn't say to him in that magic spot beside the crystal water, but here in the sunlight, in the high heat of the day, she found her voice frozen by the lack of a future for them. She couldn't offer him whatever it was he needed because she'd buried it already. And he? He hadn't offered her anything except himself, and that precious moment had passed, as well.

He drew Jezebel up abruptly and was staring ahead, rising in his stirrups, leaning forward.

"What is it?" she asked.

"The vultures are circling something up ahead."

"Oh, no," she said. "Not one of the cattle."

"Maybe," he answered. He sat in the saddle and flicked her a strange look. "You might want to hang back here. A dead or dying animal isn't anything pretty to look at."

Jeannie thought of the undertaker who'd told her essentially the same thing about her husband and daughter. And she'd believed him and hadn't gone in to say goodbye. And had been haunted ever since by the lack of certainty that they'd really gone forever and weren't in some strange witness relocation program and might reappear any day.

Though it wasn't the same, she used the memory to instill some courage. "I'm going with you," she said.

As if as uncomfortable with the way the afternoon was ending as she was, he urged his horse forward and trotted south and west.

"How many fires does *others* mean?" she asked.

"More than three, less than ten," he said. "Beyond those you had before Pablo and I came out here."

"Why didn't you tell me?"

He shifted in his saddle as if uncomfortable. And Jeannie knew he *was* uncomfortable. Not about the fires, but about something he wasn't telling her. Maybe it had something to do with what he'd tried to confess in the chasm when she'd stopped him.

Thinking about it, she realized the wonder wasn't that he was hiding something from her, nor even that she'd stopped him from telling, but that she'd felt she knew someone well enough to know exactly what he was thinking. To know someone with the kind of inner radar that allowed her to glimpse his thoughts, his needs, his wants was an intimacy she'd believed closed to her forever.

He raised on his stirrups again, everything about him alert, tense and somehow utterly dangerous.

She followed his gaze and gasped. Something was lying in the grass in the distance, something dressed in red, yellow and faded blue. Everything in her screamed a denial, but she kept silent.

When they were some twenty yards away, Jeannie knew what the something was, though she'd tried hard to convince herself it was a pile of clothing or a bunch of rags some careless person had left there.

Overhead, vultures made large lazy circles on huge wings and nasty gargling sounds issued from pink wattles on their misshapen necks. Too many movies, too much present fear managed to send a chill down Jeannie's back.

"Stay here," Chance said, reaching out a hand for one of Diablo's reins and drawing the horse to a stop. "I don't want to see this, let alone even think about you getting a close-up view." His eyes bored into hers, the first time he'd truly met her eyes since she'd screamed his name near the water of her magic pond. And in them was a far different demand there than she'd seen earlier that afternoon. A hard command.

Jeannie lifted a hand as if showing him the way. She stayed where she was, holding the reins of a restive Diablo.

Every nerve stretched tight, she watched as he moved away from her, closer to the pile of rags that couldn't be anything but a body, and again she thought of David and Angela. Maybe she'd done the right thing back then. She'd been haunted by the need to see them again, and all the literature she'd read about grieving had said this desire would ebb and flow with time and healing. But she'd at least always envisioned them whole, not broken and torn.

She chewed on her lower lip and wished for her notebook. She needed to write down some of her thoughts. It was so much easier than dealing with the blatant reality she watched unfolding before her eyes.

She watched Chance urge an anxious Jezebel forward. The horse nervously picked her way across the desert brush. When he was close to the person lying in the grass—Jeannie had no doubt that was what it was—he pulled the skittish horse to a halt, swung a leg over her back and dropped to the ground.

Jeannie had seen his eyes raking the surrounding desert as they'd approached, so she wasn't surprised to see him do so again. But this time, he transferred the reins to his left hand, and his right hovered near his hip, as if looking for a gun that should be there.

Leading Jezebel, Chance walked a broad circle around the dead man, who wore a yellow shirt, blue jeans and what appeared to be a red shawl of some kind around his neck.

Chance looked at the buzzards circling and crying raucously and uttering their gurgling babble overhead, then glanced at her. His expression was grim and not just dangerous, but deadly.

"I don't suppose you have a cell phone on you, do you?"

She shook her head. She wanted to be anywhere but

out here in this desert. She ached to be back at her magical pond. "No, I'm sorry, I don't," she whispered.

She wanted to ask if the person was dead but knew the question was naive. Of course the man was dead. Nothing could lie so still in the New Mexico sun with vile, screeching vultures flying overhead and flies buzzing around in busy activity and not be dead.

"Chance?"

"It's Jorge Martinez," he said. "Lucinda's husband. Damn. Ah, damn."

Jeannie remembered Doreen saying something about a cousin of hers whose husband had disappeared. "Oh, no," she said. A thousand questions trembled on her lips. What was the man doing on her land? How long had he been missing? What could she do to help Lucinda, Doreen's cousin? For who knew better than she did what it was to have the worst of terrible news delivered?

"What do we do?" she asked.

"We report it from the ranch," he said. "But not to the sheriff. I want you to go back to the ranch and call the federal marshal's office. Tell them I told you to call and that I want them out here right now."

"Why—?"

"Jeannie, there's no time to explain all this. I'll ride with you to the road so you won't get lost, then I'll wait for Ted and Dell out here."

"Ted and Dell?"

"Deputy marshals," he said tersely.

"I don't understand any of this," she said.

"There's more to it than that. I tried to tell you— hell, that doesn't matter now. Jeannie, this man didn't just die out here. He's been murdered."

Chance's last word reverberated through Jeannie's

soul. *Murdered.* The man hadn't wandered onto her property and succumbed to heat prostration or gotten lost and dropped from lack of water or food. The man—Jorge, husband of Doreen's cousin Lucinda—had been killed.

"How?" she asked.

"I think you can take your pick," Chance growled.

He waved off some flies—making Jeannie wince—and after a careful look around the body, stepped closer to the hapless Jorge. He knelt down and stared, not at the body, but at something lying beside it. Keeping a tight hold on Jezebel's reins, he pulled a utility knife from his jeans pocket and flipped it open. He snared something from the ground and held it carefully away from him, then studied it closely.

Jeannie couldn't tell what the object was, at first, as it made so little sense in its present context, then realized she was looking at a trophy of some kind. Gold glinted through the grime on the dust-covered trophy of a man riding a bucking horse. She didn't need to see the name on the plaque to know who the trophy belonged to.

Out of the thousand questions rushing through her, Jeannie could only focus on one. "How long has he been dead?"

"What? I don't know. Two days, maybe. Could be more. Doesn't really look like he was killed here."

Jeannie didn't ask him how he knew this. She'd asked her question only because of the children. José and Dulce were at the ranch, alone with Juanita, the sometimes present Tomás and sweet Pablo. She felt a sharp stab of alarm.

"We've got to get back to ranch now," she said. Her voice was sharp enough to make him look up from poor Jorge's body and the trophy he held by his utility knife. "Right now. We have to make sure the kids are okay."

"Pablo's there," he said. But, even as he said the appeasing words, he was rising from his crouch over the body. "They'll be okay."

"We don't know that," she said. "I know it sounds crazy, but besides this man here, something's wrong. I can feel it. Can't you?"

She could tell by his eyes that he did. She didn't have to explain it to him. He was there with her, as he had been in the magical pond. The magic still lived, still breathed. "Yes, I can feel it," he said. And his rough, corduroy voice seemed to hover over the desert every bit as much as the vultures flying above.

"Now, Chance. Please." She pulled on Diablo's reins, and he danced beneath her, ready to do her bidding but not sure what she wanted. "I don't know the way," she called.

"Wait for me," he said easily, and it sounded far more complex than a simple command. It had the alluring sound of a vowlike plea.

"I have to," she muttered.

"That'll be the day," he said, mounting Jezebel. "You're only waiting because you don't know which way to turn Diablo." And he made that mystical clicking sound only horses seemed to recognize, and Jezebel launched from a standstill into a full canter.

Jeannie didn't have to make the clicking. She nearly fell off her mount when Diablo leaped forward, unwilling to be left behind by Jezebel. The macho horse tore across the ground like a racehorse in training, strong forelegs propelling them forward while his hind hooves dug at the earth and sent it flying.

Chance rode in the lead, heading due south, his back straight, his broad shoulders—tanned shoulders she'd caressed throughout the afternoon—forward. He seemed so much a part of the horse he looked like a centaur. A man-beast with a trophy tied to his saddle.

Jeannie didn't think about her inability to ride. She didn't consider the hardness of the ground. She only thought of two vulnerable children and a man named Jorge who died on her ranch with a yellow shirt on and a red shawl around his neck.

She could barely see Chance ahead of her, though Diablo labored to close the distance between them. She tried not to think of the afternoon they'd shared. She attempted not to question what confession she'd silenced with her insistence that the pool was so magical lies were acceptable. And, most of all, she strove to keep her imagination in check so as not to picture the children hurt, damaged and, please God, not killed like poor Jorge.

Like some desert sea captain, Chance seemed to know exactly where he was, and within minutes their horses galloped to the road leading into Rancho Milagro, panting but still nervous, as if they knew why their riders had fled the hot desert.

Diablo stomped his feet and snorted while Jezebel shook her head as though trying to slough the adrenaline still pumping through her. Jeannie wished she could do the same.

"You get to the ranch. Won't take you more than five minutes, straight down the road. I'm sorry to make you do this, but I don't want—"

He bit off whatever he'd been about to say. Jeannie filled in the blanks. "You don't want anyone messing with Jorge's body."

Chance gave her a long look. "Right. So you head on out. Make that call, get Diablo to the barn and then get the kids inside. If you tell Pablo what we found, he'll know what to do. Okay?"

"Chance?" She wanted to say so many things. To warn him to be careful, to tell him she hated this ending to a perfect afternoon.

"Trust me," he said, misunderstanding her.

Trust him. His hallmark. The stamp of a man used to taking charge, saving the day. He'd put out fires on her ranch. He'd tamed children, horses, cattle, puppies and woken her comatose heart.

"I trust you," she said.

He stared at her as if she'd spoken a foreign language. His hands pulled sharply at Jezebel's reins, and she sidled into Diablo. "What did you say?"

"I trust you, Chance."

She felt she shouted it and that the hawks flying overhead called the message to each other. The sky itself should have fallen with the admission.

"Jeannie?"

"I trust you," she repeated.

"God, woman. You pick your moments, don't you?"

"Is there a better time?"

He smiled, a ragged, crooked smile that seemed more sad than happy. "God, yes," he answered honestly. "But I'll hold you to those words when I get back."

"I might forget them by then," she said, smiling at him.

"So write them down in your little notebook," he said.

Chapter 11

Chance watched Jeannie disappear in a cloud of dust. He cursed himself for not going with her. There was nothing he could do for poor Jorge, and he felt foolish waiting beside the road.

The danger they'd discovered was real and very close. Whoever had murdered Jorge had dumped the body in the middle of nowhere, and not long ago. It could have been while he and Jeannie were making love in that beautiful chasm.

He'd heard nothing, but then, he wouldn't have. Every sense he possessed had been wholly absorbed in Jeannie, in her delicate taste, her silken body, the way her laughter enveloped him like a warm blanket on a cold night.

But sometime during the day, someone had thrown Jorge onto the desert grass with no more concern, and perhaps less, than someone might discard rotting garbage. And they hadn't used a vehicle to do this. There were no tire tracks within twenty yards of the body. And no signs of a struggle.

Jorge hadn't been dead the whole time he'd been missing. He'd been held somewhere. And obviously tortured, but to what end? And what, beyond strangulation, was the significance of the red shawl around his neck?

Chance used his utility knife to once again inspect the trophy he'd tied to his saddle. That it was supposed to be on the fireplace mantel in his cheap rented house in Carlsbad wasn't the only thing disturbing about finding it beside Jorge's body in the middle of Jeannie's ranch. Chance turned it over and couldn't fail to identify the dried blood on its heavy base. He was certain a DNA test would prove the blood to be Jorge's. But why had someone gone to such lengths to link a hired hand on Rancho Milagro with a murder victim?

It was like Nando's call to Jeannie a few days earlier about the drugs. Somebody—*El Patron*—wanted him out of the picture, even if it took framing him for murder to do it. And there was only one reason someone would go to those lengths—his cover had been blown.

And since he knew none of his deputies would have done such a thing, and Pablo would rather be buried at Rancho Milagro than ever say a word, it could only mean that *El Patron,* and therefore Nando, had come across some information about him.

But why would *El Patron*'s hoodlums go to such lengths, then dispose of poor Jorge where he was unlikely to be found any time soon? Was it a cat-and-mouse game? Or was there something far more sinister and much easier to explain? Had they only dropped Jorge on the way to somewhere else, planning to use his broken body later?

Jezebel started and pawed the dirt road at Chance's sudden and involuntary pressure against her flanks. He stared down the road in the direction of the ranch. What if he was missing something and had unwittingly sent Jeannie directly into the heart of danger?

Diablo took Jeannie right to the hitching post in front of the veranda at the main house. She slid from his back and nearly fell as her trembling legs threatened to give way. But the need for urgency was stronger than her desire to gain her equilibrium.

The puppies in their little pen on the veranda barked excitedly, trying to escape their prison as she hiked the reins over the post in a rough knot. Just the sight of the pups made her feel more comfortable. Nothing could be wrong if the puppies were still happy and healthy, could it?

But Jorge's body on that desert plain, and the look on Chance's face when he'd recognized him, propelled her forward. She staggered to the steps, calling for Pablo as she ran.

The blast of icy air from inside the house hit her and made her gasp in relief. She called for Dulce and José as she crossed to the telephone. Ignoring the red flashing message light, she fumbled for the phone book, then, abandoning the effort, dialed nine-one-one and told the dispatcher she needed the number for the federal marshal's office. When the dispatcher wanted to know what her trouble was, she insisted on being connected to or given the number for the marshal's office in Carlsbad.

Though she was given the number in only a matter of seconds, she had the feeling she should have called

Doreen at the post office. In love with one of the marshals, she would have the number memorized.

Jeannie's hands noticeably trembled as she punched in the number. For a split second, she couldn't remember the deputy marshals' names, but when a woman answered and asked if she could help, Jeannie gasped, "Dell or Ted. It's an emergency."

"Dell Johnson here," a deep voice said almost immediately.

"I'm Jeannie McMunn—"

"Yes, ma'am. What's wrong?"

"Chance Salazar told me to call you. We found a dead body on my ranch. Chance says to tell you it's Jorge...Jorge Martinez. And for you to come right away. He's waiting on the ranch road so he can lead you to...to the body."

"We'll be right there," Dell said and hung up without asking any further questions.

Jeannie sagged against the wall. She fleetingly wondered if she'd have received one quarter of the swift response had she called Nando Gallegos, and decided that question wasn't even worth asking.

"Dulce! José!" Jeannie called the children's names again, walking down the hall of the bedroom wing that housed them. "Where are you kids?"

No one answered her. She hesitated outside Dulce's closed door. She knocked and, hearing nothing, turned the knob. She stared at the mess in the room blankly for a minute. In any other teenager's space, she might not even have given it a second thought, but Dulce was almost preternaturally compulsive about keeping her room tidy. It was as if she'd never had control of anything in her young life and had poured all her need for order into her immediate surroundings.

The new sketchpad Jeannie had purchased for her last time she'd gone to town lay on the floor, sheets crumpled and a footprint across a charcoal sketch of José holding one of the pups.

She flew from Dulce's room to José's messy domain. Because he lived, as many children did, in a world of chaos and scattered possessions, she could see no concrete sign of anything amiss—except his tennis shoes were there. Wherever he was, he was barefoot.

She tore down the hall to the kitchen, calling the children, Juanita and Pablo. The silence in the house was terrifying.

She stumbled to a halt inside the dining room. Lunch dishes were still on the table, though it was nearly time for supper. One of the chairs lay on its back. A glass of iced tea had been overturned, and the liquid pooled around one of the plates and on the floor beneath the table.

"No...oh, please, God, no..." Scarcely able to breathe, Jeannie moved to the kitchen. Aside from the obvious clutter of a lunch prepared and ignored, nothing seemed out of the ordinary—except that Juanita wasn't there.

Jeannie raced from the house and didn't wait to mount Diablo. She ran headlong across the large circle drive to the corral and barn, calling for the children and Pablo all the way.

Every alarm bell within her jangled discordantly as she tried telling herself her family might have disregarded chores while she was gone for so long. She shouldn't have left them, shouldn't have lingered with Chance beside a magical hidden pool, leaving her children to heaven only knew what.

The barn, dark and cool, smelled of horses, hay,

leather and...the coppery tang of blood. She heard a moan from one of the stalls and for a moment of sheer cowardice couldn't move toward the sound. But her family was in danger.

As if the notion of family imbued her veins with liquid steel, she moved toward the stall. She jerked open the heavy door and almost didn't recognize Pablo Garcia lying inside. His face was battered, and so bruised that one eye seemed permanently closed.

She knelt over him, her hands in the air above his head, afraid that any touch would cause him more pain.

He muttered something as Jeannie asked, "Where are you hurt?" A better question might have been to ask where *wasn't* he hurt?

"My shoulder. Shot," he said.

She felt a slight jolt to realize she'd been right to suspect he spoke English. "Where are the children?" she asked, even as she moved his bloodied and scraped hand to see what the damage might be.

"Rudy took them," he said. "Rudy Martinez." He swore in Spanish and stopped on a hiss when she peeled away his torn shirt from the still oozing wound. What she knew about bullet wounds wouldn't fill a thimble, she thought, dazed, but considering bloodstains on both the front and back of his shoulder, she thought the bullet had passed through him.

"Stay here," she commanded. She ran from the stall into the tack room and grabbed a handful of chamois grooming towels and a couple of the leather replacement reins. Before she dropped to his side again, she asked, "Are we talking about the sheriff's man, Rudy?"

Pablo swore as she none too gently yanked open the shirt, stuffed a folded towel down and pressed it tightly against the jagged hole in his upper right chest just below his collarbone. "Rudy. Yes. *El Patron*'s man."

"I thought he was Nando Gallegos's head deputy," she said, gritting her teeth against the sight of the gaping wound, the blood and the pain she was causing him in her rush to patch him so she could find her children.

"He's no deputy. But he's Nando's boy, too. It's the same difference." Pablo ground the words out. "*Pendejo.*"

Jeannie didn't ask for a translation. "Why did he take the children?"

"*No sé,*" Pablo said. "I don't know for sure. He wasn't too interested in sharing information with me. Seems he knew about Chance. I don't know how. Juanita…"

"What about Juanita? Is she okay?"

"She tried to stop them. She begged them to let the children go. They took her, too."

"What about Tomás?"

"That *pendejo*. He works for *El Patron*. Juanita, too, I think. Tomás has been the one starting the fires. Sometimes cutting the fences. Juanita talked about it with Rudy." He gave a rough laugh. "They were talking in English because Juanita thought I didn't understand."

Jeannie stanched the exit wound in Pablo's back, wincing as he bit off a growled curse. She looped the spare strap around his chest and cinched it every bit as deftly as she'd hitched Diablo to the post at the main house.

"Who is this *El Patron*?" she asked, pulling the strap as tight as she could manage. "And why does he want my children?"

"They came, Rudy and a couple others. We were having lunch."

"Why did they take the children? And where did these men take them?"

Pablo shifted to a half-sitting position. *"El Patron."*

"And who is this *El Patron?* Tell me Pablo," she demanded.

"He's the reason Chance and I came out here. He's a murderer. A killer. But we could never catch him. He always has someone else doing his dirty work."

Jeannie felt a chill that had nothing to do with the shadows in the air-conditioned barn work over her body. A killer? A murderer had her children? She drew a ragged breath and forced herself to think, to ask questions that might lead her to her kids. "The reason you and Chance came to work here? Start with that, please. And fast."

"Chance thought your fires and cut fences had to do with *El Patron.* And Rudy was boasting about finding some two hundred head of cattle out on the range. Claimed they were some *El Patron* had been missing."

Jeannie's head was reeling. Chance had known these things all along and hadn't told her?

"Who is Chance Salazar?" she asked coldly.

"He's a federal marshal. He's under cover here. In town, too. Nobody knows he's a Fed."

"You said this Rudy or *El Patron* must have found out about Chance. Is that what you meant? Found out he is a federal marshal?"

"Si," Pablo said. He struggled to get to his feet. Jeannie gave him her arm, though a very real part of her wanted to hit him for lying to her, for letting her children be taken, for letting her go off and leave them alone that afternoon. "Is Chance here?" he asked.

"No," she said and thought of him on the road, waiting for his deputy marshals to take them to a dead body in the middle of her ranch. She thought of the way he'd cupped her face that afternoon, the way he'd kissed her. The way she hadn't let him tell her what he was doing on her ranch. She hadn't had to fight with him over that, she reminded herself grimly. If he'd really wanted to tell her, he could have, magical spot or not.

And while he made love to her, letting the truth be stripped away every bit as readily as she'd allowed him to remove her clothing, some thugs had come onto her ranch and stolen her children. Her family.

"Get Chance," Pablo said, slumping against her. "You need him."

"Where is this *El Patron?*" Jeannie asked, ignoring him.

Pablo slid down her body, his weight too much for her to support. She knelt beside him, sorry for him but feeling no tenderness. She couldn't afford it. She had to find her kids.

She pulled his face around to hers. "Where is this *El Patron?*"

"At his ranch. It's south of here. About twenty miles."

"How do I get there?" she asked.

"Get Chance."

"The hell with Chance Salazar," she snapped. "Tell me how I can find this ranch of *El Patron*'s."

"Chance should have told you. Don't be mad at him, *señora*. He didn't want to frighten you. He wanted to help you."

"He helped me, all right," Jeannie said grimly, her anger blinding her to all his positive qualities.

"He's a good man, Chance is. The best."

Jeannie felt as if everything she'd come to believe true in this universe had been tipped upside down. Innocent children she had sworn to protect and had come to love with an intensity she'd never dreamed possible had been stolen by apparent murderers and thugs. The man she'd given her body and soul to only that afternoon had steadily lied to her and neglected to tell her that she and the children were in danger all along. And her only source of help was a dying man begging her to be lenient with the very man who had lied to her.

"I'm sorry to ask this, Pablo, but why did this Rudy leave you alive?"

Pablo averted his gaze. She lifted a hand to his bruised jaw and propelled him to face her again. "Tell me, Pablo."

"Rudy told me to say that if you want the children back, you're to go to *El Patron*'s ranch and beg for them yourself."

The words seemed to hit her with the force of a physical blow. "Do you know why he wants this?" she asked.

He shook his head. "But I think it has something to do with what Tomás burned in that bowl in the barn when Chance found him."

Jeannie didn't have to think which night that was. She could still hear the sound of the metal kitchen bowl striking the ground when she'd taken hold of Chance's shirt and pulled him to her. And she'd seen him pick it up later, when she'd watched from her bedroom window and listened to her husband's ghost warning her to be careful.

She hadn't been careful, had she? She'd trusted the

man, a federal marshal, and her children had been kidnapped.

"What else, Pablo? What else did he tell you?"

"Just you, no one else. But you can't do that. You have to get Chance. He'll know what to do."

"Right," she said. "He'll pat me on my head and tell me not to worry my empty little brain about it. And then what'll happen to Dulce and José? Where is this ranch they've been taken to? If you don't tell me, Pablo, I swear I'll finish you off with my bare hands."

He gave a ragged chuckle. "I told Chance you'd be mad."

"I'm way beyond angry," she said. "So tell me."

"South of here, off the highway. First ranch road on your right on the way to town. Big gate. Las Golondrinas." Pablo took a jagged breath. "The Swallows."

The nameless thug had probably been responsible for killing Lucinda's husband, had stolen her children for unknown reasons and was holding them at a place called The Swallows. It seemed incongruous to the point of being surreal, she thought.

"You mustn't go there alone. People go there and never come back," Pablo said. His voice was fading, his eyes lowering.

"Chance will be along presently," she said. "Or I'll see him on the road." She pushed Pablo back, settling him against a bale of hay and cushioning his head with the remainder of the chamois cloths.

"Señora," Pablo called after her.

"You'll be fine," she said, though she wasn't sure she was telling the truth.

"In the bunkhouse. Get my gun. It's in the nightstand, okay? Don't go without that Or get Chance's 't's bigger."

"Thanks, Pablo."

"*De nada.* And don't forget...it's loaded."

When Chance spied Ted, Dell and Jack pulling up in the marshal's office four-by-four Range Rover, he waved his hat to signal them and turned Jezebel to the north. He swore at himself for not telling Jeannie to have them come in separate cars. He could have sent one of them on to the ranch to check on Jeannie and the kids.

He waited until they edged the all-terrain vehicle through the bar ditch and up the rise to stop alongside him. He didn't wait for their questions. He leaned down and spoke into the opened window. "One of you has to start walking to the ranch. I sent Jeannie on alone, and I don't know if whoever killed Jorge might still be around."

Dell got out. "Guess that'd be me. Cora would kill me if something happened to Jack, and Ted here just wants to see some action. Want me to send Pablo out?"

"No." Chance waited until Dell had started for the ranch, then urged Jezebel into a gallop.

He felt a little better knowing Dell was on the way to the ranch. Not a lot better, but somewhat. He knew he'd never forgive himself if something happened to Jeannie and the kids. Pablo, too, for that matter.

He found the body without difficulty, though the sun was lower in the sky and the shadows had shifted. He had the deputies pull up a fair distance from Jorge and signaled them to get a crime kit.

"Damn," Ted said, after walking a complete circle around Jorge. "Somebody worked him over pretty good."

Jack nodded. "But he hasn't been dead for two weeks. My guess would be yesterday."

"But he was dumped here today," Chance said.

"Yeah," Ted concurred. "Nothing at him yet."

Jack said, "You know, I'm retiring here in a couple of weeks—"

"I thought I told Pablo to let you go ahead and take off now," Chance said.

"Yeah, well. Couldn't leave you in the lurch," Jack muttered. "Anyway, I was about to suggest that when I do, I'll just mosey on out to *El Patron*'s prettified ranch and shoot the lowlife down like the dog he is. Whatcha think?"

"I think Cora would kill you first, then me for letting you do it," Chance said.

"Somebody strangled him, then hit him," Ted said. "That bash on the head wasn't what killed him. Not enough blood."

"Poor Lucinda," Jack murmured.

Over the raucous calls of the vultures, Chance thought he heard a horn honking. It sounded like Jeannie's Jeep Cherokee, but that was probably his imagination. He listened more closely but couldn't hear it any longer. Imagination or not, he felt uneasy and jumped on Jezebel. "You guys stay here and do the dirty work, okay? I'm going to pick up Dell and check on the ranch."

"Okay, boss," Ted said and grinned at him.

Chance didn't feel much like grinning back. His hunch barometer had gone haywire.

Chapter 12

Jeannie pressed the power off button on her cell phone and tossed it on the passenger's seat, where it collided with Pablo's gun. The cell phone looked so tiny in comparison. She thought of Pablo's suggestion to take Chance's weapon because it was bigger. She couldn't imagine being able to carry it, if that were true.

Pablo's weapon looked every inch of deadly. Black-handled, in its padded holster, just resting on the seat it made the danger seem real and more terrifying for being beyond her comprehension.

An ambulance was on its way for Pablo, and she'd called the state police. She might have federal marshals crawling all over her ranch, but she wasn't any too pleased about that, or with one marshal in particular.

Driving at a speed far too high for a dirt road, she hardly detected the lone figure walking toward her. At first glance, she thought it might be Chance, believed for a single second he'd fallen from Jezebel and was plodding on foot to the ranch.

She gave a ragged, ironic chuckle. The rodeo rider unseated by a friendly old mare. But then, was he even a rodeo cowboy? She didn't know the answer to that. Then she saw that the man walking toward her wasn't Chance Salazar. It was a total stranger, thin and wiry.

She pulled Pablo's gun from the seat onto her lap, fumbling with the holster's strap even as she slowed the car at the man's long-armed hail.

She withdrew the pistol from its holster and held it in her lap, pointing it at the car door. She rolled the window down a scant few inches and pulled to a stop beside him.

He was older than he looked from a distance. He tipped his hat. "Dell Johnson, ma'am. We spoke on the phone."

"Yes," she said. What was he doing on foot?

As if reading her mind, he said easily, "Chance is showing Ted and Jack where Jorge's body is. He sent me on to the ranch to make sure everything is okay."

"Because he's the marshal," she said.

He looked uncomfortable for a split second, then grinned at her. "No, ma'am," he said, and his blue eyes cut to her hand, not quite hiding below the steering column. He couldn't miss the gun aimed at him. He cleared his throat. "It's because he found the body and needed to be able to lead us to it. Everything okay back there?"

"No, it is not," she said baldly. "Somebody named Rudy Martinez has taken my children and shot Pablo Garcia."

She was perversely glad to see the grin wiped from his open face. "Oh, hell," he said. "Is Pablo dead?"

"No." She blinked at him, at his too-swift assumption of death. "He's alive. He was beaten pretty badly first, then shot in the shoulder. I don't know too much more than that. I patched the wound as best I could. I've already called for an ambulance. If it gets here as quickly as you did, you won't have to wait long."

"Won't have to wait— What are you talking about?" he asked, and ignoring her weapon, reached for the locked door. He jiggled the handle. "Open the door, ma'am," he commanded softly.

Jeannie ignored him. "Pablo told me this man Rudy passed along the word that if I want to see the kids again, I have to go to Las Golondrinas and beg for them myself. So if you'll excuse me…"

"What—wait!"

"He said to come alone," she said, moving Pablo's gun to the passenger's seat but not holstering it. She saw Dell Johnson looking at the deadly weapon, an odd expression on his broad face.

"You don't want to do this," he said.

"I've never wanted to do anything more," she said. "These are my children. I'm responsible for them." Her eyes suddenly swam with tears. She blinked them away furiously. "And—I love them. I can't think of a better reason."

"What can you do?" he asked wildly. "You've got to let us—let Chance—go after him." He tugged at her door handle, and when it didn't give, tried the back seat door, only to swear when he found that locked, as well. He held out his hands as if she still had a gun trained on him. "Look, you don't know *El Patron*. You don't know what he's capable of."

"No? I know he has my children and he's probably the reason there's a dead man lying on my ranch and a wounded one in the barn. And I found out he's behind the stolen cattle, the fires and the cut fences. It seems to me he's capable of just about anything. It would have been nice had someone clued me in on all this a little sooner. Chance, for example.''

''I think it's a good idea if you stick around and talk to him about that, ma'am. You can tell him off real good. Ma'am. Jeannie. Now wait. Just think about this for a minute.'' He edged toward the front of her car.

She put the car in gear. ''Move out of the way, Mr. Johnson. I'm a lot more desperate than I might look.''

''If you'll just wait.''

She honked her horn. Dell Johnson jumped as if she'd shot him but didn't move from in front of her car. She honked the horn a second time, a long, determined blast.

''Cut that out, damn it,'' he yelled. ''I already have a hearing loss.''

''Then you'd better move,'' she called back. ''Or you're going to have a leg loss, as well.'' She felt a hysterical bubble of laughter trying to break free at her unexpectedly brazen words. At the same time, she wanted to scream at him to get out of her way. ''I'm sorry to be so blunt, but I don't care if this lunatic El Puko wants the deed to my ranch and titles to everything else I own. I'll give it to him and more just to get those children back. They're my family and mean more than heaven and earth to me. And you can tell Mr. Lying-through-his-teeth Chance Salazar that for me when you see him.'' She honked again and revved the motor as she slowly released the clutch.

Dell apparently read her intentions with accuracy, for he finally jumped out of the way. It was only as she passed him, hearing him yell something about safety, that she wondered if she really would have hit him with the car. And decided that yes, even as the notion sickened her, she probably could have done exactly that to get Dulce and José back.

She heard his voice yelling something after her and glanced in the rearview mirror. Instead of waving her back, he had his gun out, pointed away from her, and was madly pantomiming something over the top of it.

She glanced from him to the gun on the seat. And understood the deputy marshal's message. He hadn't been yelling about her safety or anyone else's, he'd been trying to warn her that the safety catch was still locked on Pablo's gun. She felt her lips curve in a grim, fierce smile and reached over to flick it off.

As she straightened, she caught movement out of the corner of her eye and, suspecting it was Chance, didn't turn to look. She tightened her grip on the steering wheel and hurled down the ranch road, an angry mama bear ready to ford anything on earth to save her cubs.

It didn't take Chance three seconds to put the picture together when he saw the cloud of road dust billowing behind the Jeep Cherokee and Dell Johnson standing in the center of the road, weapon in his hand, a look of frustration on his flat features.

"Jeannie?" Chance asked, reining Jezebel in.

"*El Patron* has the kids. Pablo's been shot—it's okay. He's alive. She says she patched him up before she called an ambulance."

Chance felt the blood draining from his face. Jeannie wouldn't understand a man like *El Patron*. Who could? The man lived outside conventional rules and accepted behavior. Jeannie, with her every emotion on her beautiful face, would be more likely to fuel *El Patron*'s cruelty than to dissuade him. "And you let her go?"

"Short of shooting her, what did you want me to do?"

"Shoot her damn tires out."

Dell shook his head. "She had that crazy snub-nosed thing of Pablo's trained on me. It wasn't till she put it down that I realized she didn't have the safety off."

"I've got to go stop her," Chance said, whirling Jezebel toward the ranch.

"Rudy told Pablo she was to come alone to Las Golondrinas, to beg for the children herself."

Chance reined Jezebel in. The blood he'd felt drain earlier surged back in his fury. "That sick bastard. I'll kill him myself."

"She said she'd give up everything for her family. She said to tell you that, along with a couple of other things."

"Like how much she loves me?"

"No... I don't recollect her saying anything even a little bit like that."

Chance snorted, held his hand out and kicked a stir-rup free. "She knows I'm a Fed, then. Pablo must have told her. Get up here, Dell. We gotta go."

Dell sprang up behind Chance, his thin frame fitting easily behind the saddle. He barely had time to take hold of Chance's belt before Chance urged Jezebel to a full gallop.

"What did she mean, her family?" Dell yelled, struggling to keep his grip on the belt and not grab Chance around the middle. "Thought this was an orphan's ranch."

"She's made them a family," Chance yelled. He heard his words at the same time Dell must have. But for him they had meaning Dell would never understand, not having shared the meals in her loving home, not having watched her struggle to overcome Dulce's prickly ways or encourage little José to join in an activity. Dell hadn't overheard her heart-wrenching story of her tragic past, nor would he ever know how utterly disarming she could be when she blurted whatever happened to be on her mind. And, if Chance had anything to say about it, Dell would never know how beautiful she was when all her clothes and guards were cast aside. As if she'd been blessed with an unusual twist on the Midas touch, everything Jeannie laid her hands upon turned to family.

Chance was off the horse only half a second behind Dell, landing a mere two feet from the bunkhouse door. He tossed his deputy the reins and barked orders to secure Pablo and get everyone to *El Patron*'s ranch as soon as possible. He was out of the bunkhouse in seconds, his .357 Magnum in hand. "Hell, call in the state cops. They can buzz the place with their helicopters, and *El Patron* sure can't own a piece of any of them."

"How do you suppose he made you?" Dell asked.

"I figure it has to be that Tomás. Twerp probably listened at keyholes. I should have gotten rid of him when I found him in the barn. Or maybe the place was bugged."

"I think we did a bunch of underestimating about this situation."

Chance couldn't agree more. A pair of blue eyes and roan-colored silk skin had made him reckless, so content to be in her presence that he'd ignored every warning sign.

"Dell, I want you to have the state guys and the local cops round up any and all of *El Patron*'s henchmen they can lay their hands on and lock them up separately so they can be broken down more easily. I don't care what excuse they manufacture to hold them. Stick every one with murder, for all I care. Until lawyers can be brought in to sort out the mess, they can be held for hours, maybe days. Short of physical abuse, use any means to make at least one of those idiots talk. You can start with the boys they collected out at the potash plant the other day.''

''I'll have them tell the thugs all about Pablo. One of them is bound to be related to him somehow.''

Chance hesitated, meeting his deputy's solemn eyes, then he leaped into his truck. ''I just want to take the creep out once and for all.''

''You know what your pretty lady called him? El Puko.''

Worried as he was, Chance gave a bark of laughter. Leave it to Jeannie, he thought, to say exactly what she was thinking. He was wryly grateful to Dell for lightening his dark fury and more than a little relieved when the engine turned over mightily and purred sweetly. Another thing Jeannie had touched.

''Chance,'' Dell called.

''What is it?''

''You better watch out for her. She's ready to die for those kids.''

''Well, that makes two of us,'' Chance said grimly. ''Because I'm sure as hell ready to die for her.''

Jeannie entered the gates of Las Golondrinas slowly, easing the Jeep across the metal cattle guard as if anticipating the pipes would spring loose and drop her into the earth.

The high wrought-iron arch she passed beneath held

ornate metal swallows crafted by a master artist. Someone had planted bright red geraniums in the large planters flanking the gate, and the road leading to the ranch was not only graded but layered with asphalt, as well.

This *El Patron* obviously had more money than he needed and was fond of creature comforts and beauty, so what could he possibly want with her? What could he hope to achieve by kidnapping her children and making her beg to have them back?

Far from the highway, after several broad, rolling hills, she arrived at a massive, two-story adobe structure. It more closely resembled a large hotel than a ranch house, and the grounds were exquisite with flowers, shrubs and tall graceful desert willows in full bloom.

Jeannie put the Jeep into park and gathered her cell phone and Pablo's gun. The phone she slipped into a pocket, the gun she held on to, after first studying it to discover how to cock it. Like a toy gun, it was simple—pull back the cock, squeeze the trigger. The first she practiced, the latter would have to wait. She hoped forever.

A dog barked nearby, but no beast ran to challenge her as she walked to the front door on shaking legs. She hoped her extreme nervousness didn't show as she raised the large knocker on the huge double doors.

Within a few seconds, a small wooden window in the right-hand door opened, and a teary-eyed Juanita gazed at her.

Jeannie gaped. She hadn't believed Pablo when he'd told her Tomás and Juanita had been involved. Jeannie was certain Juanita, at least, would never have harmed her or the children.

"I'm so sorry, *señora*. I didn't want to. I promise

you that. I—'' She cried out and jumped as if slapped, then turned her head to look behind her. She gave a half sob and closed the little window.

Jeannie raised her hand to the clangor but before she could release it a second time, she heard the sound of a lock being turned and a bar being lifted. One of the doors swung outward, nearly hitting her.

Jeannie felt dazed by what she saw inside. A wonderland of an interior courtyard was behind the door, populated with so many different varieties of flowers and low flowering shrubs that she felt dizzy from the visual splendor and the overwhelming aromas. A three-tiered fountain gurgled in the center of the courtyard, and an enormous, long-haired Persian cat lounged beneath the fountain's pedestal.

If Juanita hadn't been in tears, Pablo not bloodied and wounded in her barn, she would have imagined she'd been invited for the Spanish equivalent of high tea.

But a tearful Juanita was standing back from the entrance to the courtyard. Not trusting that the woman was alone in this amazing garden, Jeannie raised Pablo's gun and held it with both hands. Surprised at how natural the gun felt in her grip, she pointed it at Juanita's torso. ''Where are Dulce and José?''

Though her eyes widened at the sight of the gun, Juanita didn't move from her post at the door. ''They are inside, *señora*. They are safe enough for now. You are to come in.''

Jeannie barked at her. ''Move away from the door, Juanita. And whoever's behind the other one, come out, too.''

''There's no one there,'' Juanita said. She looked at the house.

Only then did Jeannie see the man standing in the shadows of a leafy tree at the far end of the garden. If he hadn't moved, she wouldn't have seen him, for the nearly setting sun striking the wall of glass reflected nothing but itself and portions of the garden. He wore a gray suit that exactly matched the cat beneath the pedestal and the trunk of the tree he stood beneath. He was a short man, and stocky, built along powerful lines. He looked as though he were ready to attend the theater. Except for the coiled whip in his hand.

"Thank you, Juanita. Now step back and let the *señora* come inside my lovely garden," he said. Although his voice was warm enough, a chill worked down Jeannie's arms. She willed herself not to think of that whip in his hands, of what he must have done to Juanita, or worse, to the children. Mostly she concentrated on keeping her hands from shaking.

"Please, Señora McMunn. There is no one hiding behind my door. Juanita, if you would be so kind, open it for her so that she can see for herself."

Jeannie's housekeeper stepped to the side without looking behind her. Her eyes were locked on Jeannie's, and she seemed to be trying to convey half a dozen messages at once. All of them spelled danger. She released some mechanism behind the door and gave it a push. It swung wide and revealed more of the wonderful garden.

"So you see, *señora,* you have nothing to fear. Besides, I see you came armed, no?" He stepped closer and waved his free hand at the pathway that would lead her into the garden.

She raised her gun—how swiftly it had ceased belonging to Pablo—and pointed it at the man. "Are you *El Patron?*" she asked.

The man chuckled, and the chill that claimed Jeannie's body transformed to ice and threatened to weaken her. "Some people call me that, my dear. But come. We must talk, you and I."

Chapter 13

Chance spent most of the twenty flagrantly speeding miles to Las Golondrinas on his cell phone organizing an impromptu raid on the ranch. His superiors in Washington had agreed to obtain a blanket warrant to be immediately filed on the man calling himself *El Patron*. It would list state and federal criminal activities as the cause for search, seizure and arrest.

The state cops told him they could be there with helicopters in just under a half an hour and to wait for them.

Thanks to Dell, the local cops had already collared two of *El Patron*'s boys at a local bar.

The last call was the easiest to make, but the request was the hardest to satisfy. He asked for and was finally granted a warrant for the arrest of one Nando Gallegos, soon to be ex-sheriff of Eddy County.

The trouble with all those lawful and legal calls was that he didn't have time to wait for any of the paperwork before storming *El Patron*'s castle. Somewhere inside it, two innocent kids and a vulnerable woman were being held hostage, and knowing *El Patron*'s handiwork, Chance knew he had to get in there quickly and get them out fast.

And the trouble with that was, how?

He'd expected closed gates and guarded roads. No barrier prevented access to the ranch. And nothing slowed his progress to the parking area, either. His heart performed a slow flip when he saw Jeannie's Jeep parked there, for all the world as if she were on a social call.

He'd told her to trust him and he'd let her down.

Not this time.

He took his gun and the cell phone, tucking the former in his belt and the latter in a pocket of his jeans. He glanced at his watch. The state police would be there in twenty minutes, Ted and Jack in less than that.

But five minutes of thinking about Jeannie and the kids alone in there with that madman seemed an eternity to Chance. He decided to brazen it out. Waltz in the front door and hope to hell he could stall things long enough for the cavalry to arrive.

"And where do you think you're going…marshal?" Rudy Martinez asked from directly behind him.

Jeannie leveled her gun at *El Patron*'s broad chest. "Where are my children?"

The urbane man raised graying eyebrows as if surprised at her rudeness. With only a trace of an accent, he said, "They are inside, as Juanita told you. She's failed me in many ways, but she invariably tells the 'ruth. Unlike her husband."

Juanita gave a choked cry and buried her face in her hands.

"None of that, now," the man said.

Jeannie had believed she'd known evil before. She'd suffered the deaths of her husband and baby daughter and thought the early morning drunk who took their lives was evil. At *El Patron*'s silken voice, somehow more a threat than an admonition to Juanita, she realized she'd never encountered true evil before. She clearly was in the presence of it now.

She wanted to demand that he get Dulce and José, but was afraid he would somehow melt into the false glass sunset and shadows and she would be left with no leverage.

Obviously unafraid of her weapon, the man called *El Patron* turned his back on her and walked toward the glass walls. Before disappearing into the illusion, he reached out and slid aside one of the glass panels. "Juanita, please, the gates, if you will. And you, *señora*, you wished to see the children. Please, follow me. Come."

Despising herself for not having the courage to shoot the glass panel beside him and demand he give up her children, Jeannie followed him, keeping the gun in front of her. She heard Juanita closing and locking the gates behind her.

The inside of his home was as incredible as the garden. Rich carpets covered highly polished red Saltillo tiled floors. Ornate furniture formed conversational areas brightened by cut flowers from the garden. An ebony grand piano nestled in a far corner of the massive room. Museum-quality artwork covered the walls.

However, no matter how beautiful the garden or the house, Jeannie couldn't help but feel that it was like decoration on a burned cake. No amount of confectioner's sugar could mask the bad taste. All the beauty in the world couldn't hide the evil in *El Patron*.

He led the way down a broad hallway at least twice the size of her large living room and opened a set of double doors. He didn't look behind him to see if she followed. He stepped inside the room and said, "Ah, children. I've brought that visitor I promised you."

"Jeannie?" she heard Dulce ask in a choked voice.

Jeannie rushed into the room, her gun raised before her.

Because he'd spoken to the children, because Dulce had replied, Jeannie had felt marginally foolish for thinking the man a creature of consummate evil. This delusion was destroyed immediately when she entered the room. He hadn't lied about the children being there. But they were far from safe.

Jeannie's heart jerked painfully in her chest at the sight of them. Both were standing on stiff Mexican caned chairs, hands tied behind their backs, and both wore thick, rough nooses around their slender necks. The nooses were attached to a thick beam hanging below the ceiling as if placed there for that purpose.

El Patron strolled to stand behind the children. He tossed his whip onto a broad marble desk then placed a hand on each of the two straight-backed chairs holding the children.

"Oh, please," Jeannie said. The gun she'd been holding with such bravado seemed to gain ten pounds, and her trembling hands could barely hold it aloft.

"Now, what do you say, my dear? Will you set that ridiculous gun down before it accidentally goes off and hurts someone?"

She couldn't bring herself to fire the gun. She wasn't

trained in weapons. If she fired at the man, she could easily miss and hit one of the kids. And if by some miracle she did manage to shoot him, he might pull the chairs down with him, hanging the children.

Her breath snagged in her throat. Everything in her screamed not to put down her weapon. But his hands tightened on the chairs, and he gave them a little rock.

Dulce screamed. José choked.

Jeannie tossed the gun to the plush carpet and mildly wondered that it didn't fire.

He stopped rocking the chairs. "Very good. I like a woman who understands me so quickly."

"What do you want?" she asked.

"Ah, and a woman who likes to get straight to the point. Even better."

"What do you want from me?" she asked. Every fiber of her being ached to snatch the children from his grasp, to pull them into her arms.

"Your ranch," he said. "That's all I want."

"Fine. It's yours."

"You see, children. I told you she would see things my way."

"Now let them go," she said.

He chuckled. "Not so fast, my dear. You take some of the pleasure out of the deal."

"What deal?"

"Why, our deal, of course."

"I don't understand. Why didn't you just buy the ranch when it was up for sale?"

He smiled and shook his head. "You're right. You don't understand, my dear. So few do. I don't buy things, *señora*. People give them to me."

"You said you wanted my ranch. I'm giving it to you. Now let the children get down from those chairs!"

Jeannie watched him, saw the feral enjoyment of her predicament in his eyes, and her heart filled with despair. Until she'd voiced the demand, she'd truly believed there was some way to get the children safely away from him. But her statement let her know how incredibly naive she'd been to think so. He would take the ranch and kill them anyway, all of them.

"It's my ranch by rights," he said. "My great-grandfather on my mother's side was given all the land you can see from the top of the Guadalupes to the border of Mexico."

"Then how—"

"How was it taken from my family? It's very simple, *señora*. When the New Mexico Land Office opened, they claimed most of the grants null and void and stole the land from me. Now the government is paying attention to some of the old grants. I had the original deed, you see."

She didn't, but nodded anyway.

"Did you notice that I used the past tense?" He gave her a swift smile. "You're very perceptive. Yes, I said I had the deed. Tomás stole it from me. He was supposed to light fires, to scare you away, you see, but instead he steals from *El Patron* and lights an heirloom on fire. And do you want to know why he did it?"

He rocked the chairs again, and the children cried out as they struggled for footing.

"Stop it!" Adrenaline coursed through her body, making her feel ill from enforced inaction. She'd never felt so helpless. Just standing there, watching a madman torture two innocent children, was the hardest thing she'd ever done. But he could kill one or both with a single movement of his manicured hands.

He set the chairs to the floor. "He did it because he

liked you, *señora*. And because he liked the children. He didn't mind lighting the fires or cutting your fences when Rudy told him to do so, but he didn't want you to leave such a noble project. So you see why I was angry with Tomás. It made Juanita sad, but it couldn't be helped.''

"You can have the ranch," Jeannie said.

"No!" Dulce cried. "You can't do it. He's lying, anyway." She cursed at him as her chair was rocked again.

"I thank you, *señora*. I accept your kind offer. I have a contract for deed right over here."

She would sign away her soul if it would get him away from those chairs and the lives so dangerously teetering on them. It didn't matter that it wouldn't be legal without Leeza and Corrie's signatures, anyway.

"It was very distasteful to me to take matters into my own hands, but you made the mistake of hiring a federal marshal as a ranch hand. That we had one in the area I knew. I just didn't know who it was until Tomás told me, the night he saw equally pathetic Jorge die right in front of him. Then he was willing to tell me many things he overheard on your ranch."

"I don't know what you're talking about," she said carefully. "If you'll just let me sign the deed, we can go."

"Now wait a minute," he said, as if he'd thought of something almost impossible to contemplate. "What is to stop you from going to the police the minute you leave here?"

"My promise," she said.

"Ah, yes. A woman's promise. That is very important, is it not? But I think these dear children could tell you that women often break their promises, no? Still, if I did believe you, how would I trust you?''

Jeannie thought of what she'd said to Chance, that she trusted him. He'd said to write it down in her notebook. She hadn't trusted him, though. The very hour she'd uttered the words, after she learned he had lied to her, she hadn't waited for his advice on how to get the children back safely. She hadn't trusted him to do what was right. They might all die because of her lack of faith.

''I don't know,'' she said honestly, wearily.

''I can't think of a single way, either.''

''I can.'' Dulce spoke unexpectedly.

El Patron chuckled. ''What's that, dear girl?''

''Chance comes and kills you for all the bad things you've done to people and then we don't have to worry about who you will and won't trust, now will we, *pendejo?*''

''Dulce!'' Jeannie cried, afraid the girl would goad *El Patron* into pulling over her chair.

Instead, the monster laughed. ''She has spirit, this one. I have a place in Mexico that can use her.''

When Rudy stopped him, calling him marshal, he fully expected a bullet in his back. *El Patron*'s chief henchman, a notch higher than Nando, Rudy could easily be considered a psychopath. He had no feelings for human suffering.

But Rudy Martinez was also a coward. The only feelings he did suffer from were fear-related. Chance knew this from long experience with Rudy, and all the Rudies of the world. Without his buddies to help him bully others, Rudy might easily be subdued.

So when the bullet didn't plow through his back,

Chance whipped around and slammed his .357 across Rudy's face. The man went down like a sack of moldy oats.

"That was for Pablo," he said, bending over the man.

He dragged him to the pickup's rear bumper and shoved him roughly to the ground. "That was for Jorge."

He pulled a set of handcuffs from a small satchel in his pickup and wasn't gentle as he snapped them around Rudy's wrists. "That was for taking the kids."

He tore off a strip of duct tape and covered Rudy's mouth with it, making sure the thug's moustache was good and covered. "And that's for scaring Jeannie."

Feeling much better and with a slight smile on his face despite his worry, Chance again headed for *El Patron*'s heavy wooden gates.

He didn't feel quite as confident when he approached a wide-open front gate. The setting sun provided enough light for him to see inside the gates easily. It was a riot of flowers and trees and shadows broad enough to hide an army in.

He abandoned the bold approach and slid into the shadows, drawing his gun and moving slowly across the courtyard to an open glass door.

He nearly shot Juanita when she stepped from behind a huge potted plant and put her finger to her lips. She leaned close to whisper in Spanish in his ear. "The others are all asleep. I put something in their soup. Except for Rudy. He wouldn't eat and I can't find him. *El Patron* has the *señora* and *los niños* in a room down the hall."

"You don't have to worry about Rudy. I met him

down below. Are they okay?'' Chance whispered in English.

Juanita shook her head. "He has the children on chairs and ropes around their necks. He holds the *señora* in place when he rocks the chairs."

Horrified at the mental image she created and mystified by her presence, he peered at her more closely. She'd obviously been crying, and when he patted her shoulder, she flinched in pain.

"You might want to hide," he said. "In case one of the others comes back."

"No, I stay for the *señora*."

"Then wait outside the gate. My men will be coming soon. Stay away from the pickup. Rudy's handcuffed to the bumper."

Tears welled in Juanita's eyes. *"Dios Mio."*

He frowned. Was this a trap of some kind?

She shook her head as if he'd asked the question aloud. *"El Patron* killed Tomás."

Chance winced. He hadn't liked the man, but he certainly hadn't wished him dead.

"Me? I help to kill *El Patron.* Then maybe God will forgive me and let me go to heaven when I die."

"Wait down by the courtyard gates," Chance said, unable to think of any words of solace for the widow of a man who would burn a woman's ranchland and endanger children. Although her words had shocked him somewhat, he knew exactly how she felt. If anything happened to Jeannie or the kids, he'd kill *El Patron* personally. And with pleasure.

He looked at the expanse of Saltillo tile and paused long enough to remove his boots before creeping down the hall, looking for his family.

* * *

"Why are you doing this?" Jeannie asked the man. She fought tears of frustration and fear. She would not cry in front of this monster. She suspected this would be a man who would enjoy seeing someone cry and relish driving them to tears.

"You ask me why I do this? Because I can, *señora*. Just because I can."

"Not this," she said. "You can't get away with this."

"I can get away with anything," he said. "Did you notice my garden? How beautiful it is? It's because I fertilize it with the bodies of my enemies. Look at these beautiful children, for example. No one but you will miss them. And no one would ever look for them here."

"I've already called the state police," Jeannie said.

"Oh, they are no trouble. I'll have Nando steer them away. He'll arrest someone for stealing your little orphans no one will find, and that someone will take the blame. Maybe even Nando himself. He's been annoying me lately, anyway. Or no, I have a better idea. Let's arrange things so that your cowboy, Chance Salazar, takes the credit. He's a rodeo cowboy gone crazy with love for a pretty face, but he's insane, so he kills everyone at the ranch. I like that story, don't you? Of course, he might be a federal marshal, and in this play, he accidentally kills the children—and you, of course—to cover up his murder of Jorge and Tomás. Naturally, I will have tried so hard to rescue you. I will be inconsolable." He sighed heavily. "And I would still have your ranch. You see, there are so many ways to take care of a garden, *señora*."

Dulce made a strangled sound, and Jeannie instinctively stepped forward. *El Patron* stopped her by placing his hand on Dulce's chair and giving it a wiggle. Even as Dulce cried out and danced on the chair's seat, Jeannie was, for the first time, aware the girl was grimacing not in pain, but as a warning of some kind.

She was able to see something Jeannie could not. And *El Patron,* behind the girl, apparently couldn't see it, either.

Jeannie's heart began to beat in a rapid, hopeful rhythm.

El Patron stopped the chair torture.

"Are you a gardener, *señora?*"

"She's a great gardener," Dulce said. Her eyes rolled toward the door to the hallway. "Chance helped her." Dulce's eyes went from the door to Jeannie and back to the door. "He stood right behind her every day and told her where to plant stuff."

And Jeannie knew that somehow, miraculously, Chance was there. He'd come for them. She felt galvanized by hope, by faith in a future, by the exultant grin on Dulce's face.

"But no doubt he didn't fertilize it with his enemies' blood. Flowers are all carnivorous, you know."

"No, only pigs like you," Dulce said, and kicked out at him.

"No!" Jeannie screamed, lunging forward and pushing *El Patron* aside as he shoved Dulce's chair over. She caught the girl around her legs before Dulce could reach the end of the rope, praying she didn't accidentally knock into José's chair as she staggered under the surprising weight.

El Patron, angered and startled by the abrupt turn of events, regained his footing and grabbed his whip from the marble desk.

"I don't think so, pal," Chance said, stepping out of the shadows into the room.

"You can't stop me," the megalomaniac said.

"Yeah? Watch this." And with that, Chance fired his gun at *El Patron*'s whip hand. The whip flew out of it as *El Patron* screamed.

Two more gunshots, and Dulce sagged into Jeannie's arms and José collapsed on the chair. For half a second, she feared he'd shot them, too, but then she saw the ropes dangling from their shoulders. Her peripheral vision let her see Chance forcing a still screaming *El Patron* onto his desk.

"Pretty good shooting, Tex," Jeannie said mildly, working at the knots of Dulce's and José's bonds.

"Yeah, all us federal marshals can do that."

He surprised a chuckle out of her, and she looked up to find Dulce, white-faced and wide-eyed, staring at Chance.

The long arm of the law had the much shorter *El Patron* in a death grip against the marble desk. The man might be evil and able to avoid prosecution thus far, but he was no match for Chance. His face was turning purple.

Jeannie watched in dazed detachment for a few seconds. She heard yelling from somewhere in the house and the sound of helicopters overhead. "Chance," she said. Then, louder, "Chance."

Chance heard her saying his name, but between an overdose of adrenaline and a burning desire to rid the world of one of its worst monsters, he was having a difficult time answering her. He flicked a glance in her direction and realized, seeing her pallor, he wasn't thinking like a marshal but rather like a distressed father upon finding his wife and children in jeopardy. As if something inside of him broke, he understood that a man—most men, in fact—could be both. Could have both.

In that brief if intense revelation and the meeting of their gazes, Chance found he couldn't read her expression. Slowly releasing the pressure on *El Patron*'s neck, he ached to be able to talk with her alone, to explain the reasons he didn't tell her about his undercover mission and his desire to protect her without her knowing danger existed. He wanted to tell her how terrified he'd been for her, for the children. He wanted to tell her how brave he thought she was and how much he longed to hold her as tightly to his breast as she held the children to hers.

"Chance, you have to stop now," she said primly. "Think of the children."

"What?"

"The children. You're their role model, you know. Our hero. And heroes can't go around killing people just because they tried to kill us."

Chance eased his hold on the purple-faced *El Patron*. "You can't? You're sure?"

"No. It's just not done. It's against the undercover federal marshal's code."

She saw the beginnings of a smile breaking through.

"Ah, and what is done?" he asked, stepping back from the desk.

Dell drawled from the doorway, "If it were me, boss, I'd let my deputy cover the guy while I kissed the girl."

"Is that what you recommend?" Chance asked José. José giggled and nodded.

"And how about you?" he asked Dulce. She grinned and shrugged.

Chance turned to Jeannie. "Seems unanimous."

She grinned at him. "Then you better kiss me and get it over with."

"Oh, I'll never be over this," he said, drawing her into his arms and pulling her to his chest. "Never." His lips lowered to hers, and he thought no kiss had ever been as sweet. But he was willing to try several more just to be certain.

Chapter 14

Huddled with the children on a sofa in *El Patron*'s huge living room, Jeannie told her story several times for various local, state and federal officers. She kept an arm around each child and was pleased beyond reason when Dulce sighed and laid her head on her guardian's shoulder.

Both children were pale and both wore rope-burn necklaces. Jeannie thought of the bruises on *El Patron*'s neck after Chance had choked him and thought the man's collar was highly appropriate.

Chance sat on the large coffee table facing them. He gave Jeannie a swift if somewhat tired smile before turning to Dulce. "I haven't had much of an opportunity to tell you what an incredibly brave thing you did back there. You may want to consider a career in martial arts or even law enforcement."

"After art school," Dulce said drowsily. "Jeannie thinks I can go to a good one."

"So do I," he said. "But keep up the kickboxing."

He patted her leg and turned to José. "And you, kiddo, what about you? How did you manage to stay on that chair with all the scuffling going on?"

José looked at him steadily for a long moment then lowered his eyes.

Chance reached out and cupped the boy's chin with his hand. "*Mi hijo,* are you going to be okay?"

Jeannie could see Chance's hand was shaking a little and his voice was rough and uneven. He'd called the boy his son. *Mi hijo...*

José lifted his gaze to Chance, then lifted his little hand to the large calloused one still holding his face. And said clearly and with great dignity, "If you call me your son, can I call you *mi papá?*"

Jeannie had to close her eyes against the sudden spasm of wonder and pain that crossed Chance's face. She held her breath, waiting for an answer, trying to withhold her cheer for the boy's talking and her fear of Chance's reply.

"I think we have much to talk about, you and me," Chance said, his voice even more jagged than before.

"I think so, too," José agreed, nodding solemnly.

Dulce wiped her eyes. "You know what I liked about today?"

"What?" José asked, as if there had never been a time he hadn't spoken.

"*El Patron* screaming like a girl."

They all giggled a little hysterically, José the loudest.

Ted Peters, a tall, dark football player of a man, came in with the news that Pablo was doing fine in the hospital and that Nando Gallegos had been arrested. "He spilled every frijole he could think of and added a few tortillas for fun." His face grew somber and he said, "I've got to go call Doreen. She's gonna be pretty upset when she hears about her cousin."

Chance winked at Jeannie before pushing to his once again shod feet. "Plus she'll need some consolation about Jorge."

Ted brightened. "That's right, she will."

"Look, I hate to do this, Ted, but do you think you could go over and tell her personally?"

Ted gave him a sharp, suspicious look that Chance met blandly.

Ted asked, "Are you serious?"

"I'm dead serious. I never kid about arrest or death notifications. Besides, we're crawling with police here. We've got *El Patron* dead to rights this time. Kidnapping, attempted murder, not to mention solicitation to murder, theft and a few hundred other things."

"Okay, then. If you say so. You're the boss."

"Get going," Chance said. "And haul Jack into town with you. Make sure Cora knows he wasn't shot at, okay?"

After Ted left and Chance had taken a long look at José and Dulce in Jeannie's arms, he tapped Dell on the shoulder and asked if he'd mind seeing the family back to the ranch. "They're done in. And I won't be finished here for a while yet. The border patrol guys want to check into this garden story of his to see if that's where some of their agents might be found. And I sure don't want Jeannie and the kids to see any of that."

Chance wasn't surprised Dell shuddered, but all the man said was, "Your pickup?"

"No, take Jeannie's Jeep. I'll send you home in my pickup when I'm done here, or you can crash out here."

Chance didn't have more time than to give each of the Rancho Milagro party a quick hug before Dell whisked them out the door. He felt odd watching them leave without him. He was near to bursting with pride in them, in their resilience, in their strength and in the budding love they were so willing to reveal.

Every time he thought about the three of them in *El Patron*'s clutches and how close he had come to losing them, he had to draw a deep breath to quell the shakes.

"Chance?" One of the state police officers called from the garden.

When he got outside, a weeping Juanita was huddled beneath the tree, a sodden handkerchief clutched in her hand. She was staring at a patch of overturned soil, flowers and a fat gray cat that sat on the mound of dirt, grooming itself.

"We've got something here," the officer said. "The lady says this is where her husband was buried. They made her watch. It's a wonder any of you got out of here alive, let alone had such an easy time of it."

Chance met Juanita's eyes. An easy time? He'd suffered every torment known to man just thinking of Jeannie and the kids in this evil place. And what Juanita had suffered, however much she might have been an unwilling participant in the early harassment of Rancho Milagro, didn't bear scrutiny.

"Go easy on her," Chance said. "If she hadn't drugged the rest of *El Patron*'s people, we probably wouldn't be here."

"Are you going to prosecute her?"

"Not if I can help it," Chance said. "I think she's been through enough. She has family down in Mexico that will take care of her. Especially now that *El Patron* can't hold them over her head."

Juanita began crying again, covering her face with her hands. Chance's cell phone rang. His heart gave a little jump when he saw Jeannie's number.

"*Vaya con Dios,*" Chance said softly to Juanita before walking into the house. Go with God.

He answered the phone. "Chance here."

"Dell. They're safe. We're at the ranch. Jeannie's cleaning up the dining room and kitchen. The kids are already in bed. They're in together. That Dulce is quite a piece of work. She wouldn't let the kid out of her sight for a second. I see what you mean about a family. She treats them like a little brood hen protecting her favorite chicks."

Chance smiled, thinking of the Dulce he'd first met, Miss Quiñones to you. "You want to take Jeannie's Jeep and head home?"

"Naw. I think I'll give your lady a hand in the kitchen and hang out here until you get back. The horses are hungry, and you've a bunch of puppies that are demanding a little attention. How did Doreen talk you into so many of them?"

Chance grinned then sobered quickly. "Juanita showed the state boys where they buried her husband."

"Jesus."

"And what about Jorge?"

"He was off to the morgue with the ambulance that carried Pablo into town. Pablo's still cursing me. And he said to tell you that he quits the marshal's office. He's staying on here as ranch hand. It's a lot more exciting, he says."

Chance chuckled. "You take care of them for me, Dell."

"As if they were my own, Chance. As if they were my own."

* * *

Jeannie heard the end of Dell's conversation with Chance and her heart warmed at his last remark, knowing that Chance had asked him to watch out for them. She thought of the first day she'd seen him, running into him on the street and having the fleeting feeling he was protecting her. She remembered the night she'd watched him in the darkness, staring at her window, and how she'd known he was up and guarding her.

Something about the memories made her want to cry. Made her want to move into Chance's arms and stay there forever.

She continued clearing the dining table and mopping up the spilled iced tea, trying not to think of the past several terrifying hours. So far, she hadn't succumbed to the hysteria lurking in her, though she knew from her background that some kind of reaction was inevitable.

She'd already checked on Dulce and José twice. Incredibly, as Dell had told Chance, both children were sleeping soundly, albeit in the same room and with a night-light on. Either the amazing strength that all children possessed was at work there, or more sadly, both children had already been through so much that a life-threatening event was just one more notch on their already scored belts.

José hadn't talked any further since his miraculous few words with Chance, revealing nothing of how he'd come to be on the ranch, who his real parents might be, or anything of his past. It seemed his desire for speech centered on the man he'd chosen as his papa.

Jeannie's eyes again filmed with tears. Would Chance even be willing to take on such a role? He hadn't answered the boy directly. His endearment to the boy may have been nothing more than just a phrase, a simple slip of the tongue. Oh, but how she wished it could be true!

"Let me do that," Dell said, taking the mop from her hands.

Jeannie gave up the handle gratefully. "Thanks for everything, Dell," she said. "And I'm sorry about holding Pablo's gun on you earlier."

He flashed her a grin. "You had me going there for a while. I saw at *El Patron*'s house that you'd taken the safety off."

"Thanks for the tip."

"This is a great place you have here," he said. "Chance told me you've made all the people here into a family. I can see why."

"Thank you, what a lovely thing to say," she said. Chance had said she made all the people at the ranch into a family. Did that include him?

"You're in love with him, then?" he asked.

Her body seemed to still. Was that what she was? In love with Chance Salazar?

"You don't have to tell me," he said. "I just thought the way you two were looking at each other..."

It was unfair to make Dell suffer embarrassment. "I don't know how I feel about Chance. I think I'm afraid of wanting too much."

"You know, my old grandmother used to say that wanting too much is never a problem, it's not wanting enough that causes the heartache."

Jeannie stopped wiping the table and looked at him. That's what she'd felt in the magic pool with Chance. And that's what she'd been afraid of with Dulce. "Your grandmother was a wise woman."

He grinned at her. "She still is, she just doesn't talk so much anymore."

Jeannie chuckled. "And you, Dell?"

"I figure I'm holding out for one of your partners," he said. "If they're anything like you, I know I could probably want a whole hell of lot." He busied himself mopping for a few fast and, she suspected, blushing minutes, then said, almost offhandedly, "You could do a lot worse than Chance. He's a good man to have around in a pinch. Besides, he's tip over teakettle for you."

Jeannie smiled. She liked the playfulness of the phrase and wished she could believe it were true, believe it enough to trust her heart to Chance, to trust her heart to anyone again.

But she did, didn't she? She'd given her heart to Dulce and to José. She hadn't railed at *El Patron*, Dell or even Pablo because the children had been her responsibility or under her care at the time of their kidnapping. She'd called them her children because that's exactly how she thought of them and how she wanted to think of them. Possessive, loving, motherly.

"Chance had some hard times as a kid. Not financially. His family has enough money to float a boat. He just never really had what I'd consider a family life. They all came and went at odd times and didn't see much of one another."

Jeannie thought of the nightly dinners and how enlivened they were by Chance's presence. How everything seemed better and easier and more fun when he was around.

Jeannie, honey, go for it. It's the right time.

She looked up, startled. It wasn't Dell's voice she'd heard. It was David's.

You can't have a future unless you let go of the past.
Her words? David's?

"I'm going to go bed down the horses," Dell said.
"And feed the pups." He gave her an odd look.

"Fine," Jeannie said absently. Her heart was pounding almost painfully in her chest. She heard the front door gently close behind Dell.

Trust yourself, Jeannie. It's not enough to trust someone else. You have to trust you first. Remember?

"David?" she whispered.

There was no answer.

Or perhaps there was, for minutes later she heard Chance's pickup truck pull into the drive.

Chance felt as if he'd traveled a hundred years that day. He'd gone from a stiff stranger with Jeannie that morning, still smarting from the night before, to as ardent a lover as was humanly and emotionally possible, to dedicated cop, to raging father and husband. He was still choked by the emotions he'd felt at seeing his new family in danger and enraged at all the harm one madman had caused over the years.

And now he was home. At least it felt like home, the first real home he'd ever known, despite having a sprawling family.

Dell greeted him, having stripped down and given a quick curry to the horses. "They're eating now and drinking about half the water left in the Pecos River," he said.

"Thanks for everything, Dell," Chance said, clasping his deputy's shoulder.

"You're a lucky man, Chance."

"I've always thought so," Chance said, dropping his

hand from his friend's shoulder. "But I gotta admit, I'm pretty nervous right now."

"Because you're gonna ask her to marry you?"

"Hell, I haven't even gotten around to telling her how I feel yet, let alone talking about marriage."

"No time like the present, pal."

Chance sighed.

"Scared?"

"Spitless."

Dell chuckled. "Well, I gotta tell you, Chance, you'd be making the mistake of a lifetime if you don't tell her just how crazy you are about her and if you don't get down on that bum knee of yours and beg her to stay with you forever. She's what my old grandmother used to call a keeper."

"Your grandmother is only in her sixties and dances in a chorus line on a cruise ship."

"She used to say it before she took to the road."

Chance grinned.

"Grandmothers aside, you gotta tell her."

"I'll remember this some day," Chance said. "And give you grief."

"You can name your first kid after me."

"Looks like it'll have to be my third."

Jeannie found herself standing tensely by the sofa in the living room, her hands clenched in her pockets. She'd heard the sound of her Jeep leaving the ranch and smiled at Chance's high-handed disposal of her property. Just as he'd gotten rid of Rudy Martinez the day they fought the fire together and the way he'd dispatched *El Patron*.

But she didn't know what to expect when he walked in the front door.

The door opened and he stood there, silhouetted against the porch light shining on the veranda. He slowly removed his cowboy hat and ran a hand through his hair. And she realized he was just as nervous as she was.

He hung his hat on the rack she'd had Pablo mount by the door soon after they arrived at the ranch, then he turned and held out his arms.

It was that simple.

She melted into them without consciously having crossed the room. He held her fiercely to him, as if trying to pull her inside his body.

"I love you, Jeannie McMunn," he said. Simply. Naturally. And with such emotion in his voice that the rough corduroy tore.

"And I love you, too, Chance Salazar," she said.

He stilled completely, as if she'd told him to clear off the place instead of returning the love he'd offered her.

"Are you having a heart attack?" she asked.

He gave a ragged chuckle and kissed her with an intensity that stole her breath. When he pulled back for air, he stroked her hair, her face and held her away from him as if memorizing her. "Dell told me I should get down on one knee."

"Does that mean I have to also?" she asked, smiling despite tear-filled eyes.

"You'd probably have to. I've got a bum knee from riding rodeo. I probably wouldn't be able to get back up again."

"Are you offering me damaged goods?"

"Yep. And you're gonna take 'em, too." He grinned at her. The smile slipped from his face. "Because I can't live without you, Jeannie. I think I've dreamed about you since I was a kid, wanting that roan Appaloosa.''

"You're such a romantic," she said.

"So, Jeannie McMunn who courts trouble and forgives a lying dog of an undercover marshal...will you marry me and be my love forever?"

He's a good man, Jeannie.

"Forever's a long time," she said.

"Not long enough when you're around," Chance said, kissing her cheeks, stroking her neck, her back. "Forever doesn't seem near enough time. So will you marry me?"

"What about your job as marshal? Don't you normally work somewhere else? Albuquerque or Dallas?"

"A federal marshal can call his own station. One of the perks. I pick here. So, will you marry me?"

"I come with children. Two at least."

"I know. I figure they won't mind switching last names. And in José's case, he'll get one finally. So, will you marry me?"

"And I have lots of baggage from the past," she said.

"I've a couple suitcases of my own. What do you say we stack them in the closet? We can explore them together someday. Will you marry me, damn it?"

She grinned at him. "When you put it that way, yes."

Chapter 15

Jeannie spread a thick blanket on the sandy beach in the chasm she'd named *Piscina Milagro,* Miracle Pool. Chance set down a large picnic basket Jeannie's friends Leeza and Corrie had stocked following the short wedding ceremony they'd flown out from D.C. to attend.

"Are you sure this is what you want for a honeymoon?" Chance asked.

"I'm sure," Jeannie said. "We have sky, fresh water and a private beach. What more could anyone ask for?"

Chance stretched out beside his wife of two hours. "You know, don't you, that there used to be a legend about a magic spring on this ranch somewhere."

"Pablo was saying something about that this morning."

"No one's been able to find it for more than a hundred years."

"We did."

"It makes wishes come true," he said.

Jeannie looked at him and felt her heart would over-flow with the love she felt for him. "I made a wish the first day I found this place," she said softly. "I wished I could just open up to you. To love you."

"And I made a wish when we came here together," Chance murmured, drawing her down to nestle in his arms. "I wished that I could hold you forever."

"And now we're here."

"In a place where wishes come true."

"Chance?"

"Yes, love," he said.

"One of us must have made another wish that day," she said.

"I'm sure I made a few. I think this is one of them." He unfastened her blouse and laid it open. She was a continual marvel to him. He pressed a kiss to her collarbone and trailed it with his tongue.

"Remember when we were here before?"

"Oh, yes," he said, and proved he did.

"And you told me you were safe?"

He stiffened a little. "Are we bringing out some baggage here on our honeymoon?"

"No...not baggage. Package, maybe."

He hiked up on one elbow and stared at her. "What are you telling me, Jeannie?"

"We weren't safe from having a baby."

"You're having my baby?"

"I am."

"Well, that's just fine then," he said, settling back down. "But I have to warn you, Dell says we have to name it after him."

"As long as we don't have to name it after his grandmother."

"I love you, Jeannie Salazar."

"And I love you, Chance Salazar."

"So, what are we going to wish for today?"

"How about this?" she asked.

"Oh, I like that wish. How about this one?"

"That's good, too."

"And this?"

"Just perfect," she sighed. "Absolutely perfect."

* * * * *

CODE NAME: **DANGER**

The action continues
with the men—and
women—of the
Omega Agency in
Merline Lovelace's
Code Name: Danger
series.

This August, in
TEXAS HERO (IM #1165)
a renegade is assigned
to guard his former
love, a historian whose
controversial theories
are making her sorely in
need of protection. But
who's going to protect
him—from her? A couple
struggles with their past
as they hope for a future....

And coming soon, more
Code Name: Danger stories
from Merline Lovelace....

Code Name: Danger
Because love is a
risky business...

**Where royalty and romance
go hand in hand...**

The series continues in Silhouette Romance
with these unforgettable novels:

HER ROYAL HUSBAND
by Cara Colter
on sale July 2002 (SR #1600)

THE PRINCESS HAS AMNESIA!
by Patricia Thayer
on sale August 2002 (SR #1606)

SEARCHING FOR HER PRINCE
by Karen Rose Smith
on sale September 2002 (SR #1612)

And look for more Crown and Glory stories in
SILHOUETTE DESIRE starting in October 2002!

Available at your favorite retail outlet.

Discover the secrets of
CODE NAME: DANGER
in
MERLINE LOVELACE'S
thrilling duo
DANGEROUS TO KNOW

When tricky situations need a cool head, quick wits and a touch of ruthlessness, Adam Ridgeway, director of the top secret OMEGA agency, sends in his team. Lately, though, his agents have had romantic troubles of their own....

UNDERCOVER MAN & PERFECT DOUBLE

And don't miss
TEXAS HERO
(IM #1165, 8/02)
which features the newest OMEGA adventure!

*If you liked this set of stories, be sure to find
DANGEROUS TO HOLD.
Available from your local retailer
or at our online bookstore.*

INTIMATE MOMENTS™

presents:

Romancing the Crown

With the help of their powerful allies, the royal family of Montebello is determined to find their missing heir. But the search for the beloved prince is not without danger—or passion!

Available in August 2002:
SECRETS OF A PREGNANT PRINCESS
by Carla Cassidy (IM #1166)

When Princess Samira Kamal finds herself pregnant with a secret child, she goes under the protection of her handsome bodyguard— and finds herself in danger of falling in love with the rugged, brooding commoner....

This exciting series continues throughout the year with these fabulous titles:

Available only from Silhouette Intimate Moments at your favorite retail outlet.

Silhouette®
Where love comes alive™

Visit Silhouette at www.eHarlequin.com

SIMRC8

If you enjoyed what you just read,
then we've got an offer you can't resist!

Take 2 bestselling love stories FREE!
Plus get a FREE surprise gift!

COMING NEXT MONTH

INTIMATE MOMENTS

SIMCNM0702